School Friends

Secrets, hopes and dreams...
School friends are for ever!

Collect the whole **School Friends** series:

Party at Silver Spires
Dancer at Silver Spires
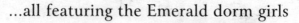
Dreams at Silver Spires
Magic at Silver Spires
Success at Silver Spires
Mystery at Silver Spires
...all featuring the Emerald dorm girls

First Term at Silver Spires
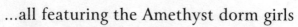
Drama at Silver Spires
Rivalry at Silver Spires

Princess at Silver Spires
Secrets at Silver Spires
Star of Silver Spires
...all featuring the Amethyst dorm girls

Want to know more about **School Friends**?
Check out
www.silverspiresschool.co.uk

Dreams
at
Silver
Spires

Ann Bryant

USBORNE

To Valerie Wilding, with lots of love,
and thanks for your humour and wisdom.

First published in the UK in 2010 by Usborne Publishing Ltd.,
Usborne House, 83-85 Saffron Hill, London EC1N 8RT, England.
www.usborne.com

Copyright © Ann Bryant, 2010

The right of Ann Bryant to be identified as the author of this work has
been asserted by her in accordance with the Copyright, Designs and
Patents Act, 1988.

Cover illustration by Rui Ricardo for folioart.co.uk

The name Usborne and the devices ♀ ⊕ are Trade Marks of
Usborne Publishing Ltd.

A CIP catalogue record for this book is available from the British Library.

JFMAMJJASON /09 95197 ISBN 9780746098660
Printed in Reading, Berkshire, UK.

Chapter One

"**O**uch!"

What's Bryony doing attacking me like this? She's supposed to be my best friend. I stopped staring at the cloudy grey sky through the gap between the treetops, and raised my eyebrows at her in a vague kind of way.

"Ems, come back from whatever planet you're on!" said Nicole, laughing. "We've been trying to attract your attention for ages!"

And when I looked round I saw that it wasn't only Bryony and Nicole who were finding me amusing, but all of my little group of friends.

"What were you daydreaming about, anyway?" asked Sasha.

It was true I'd been miles away, thinking about my other best friend, my beautiful horse, Barney, who lives back home in Ireland. I was imagining myself galloping him across open fields on a beautiful summer evening when all the work on our farm had been done – well, all the work *I* had to do at least, because Mum and Dad and my big brother Will always work till really late in the summer.

But how could I explain all that to my friends? None of them have got much of a clue about horses, and they certainly don't know the first thing about farming. I still love them dearly, though, because the six of us have been together in the same dormitory here at Silver Spires Boarding School for Girls for a term and a bit now, and the others don't seem to mind that I'm always either daydreaming or, if you press my other button, rushing to get out in the fresh air. They're not bothered that I don't care about fashion or that I'm not the best in the world as far as lessons are concerned. They all just accept the way I am. Well, apart from a few times like right now, when I think I *do* get on their nerves.

But I always know how to bring them round. "I was daydreaming about winning the lottery and just wondering which friends I might take with me on my trip to see the wonders of the world!"

That had exactly the effect I expected. Izzy and Sasha stopped trying to keep warm by jogging on the spot and gave me big beaming smiles, while Antonia and Nicole both shuffled close to me and linked their arms through mine, and Bryony started batting her eyelashes about two centimetres away from my face in a totally over-the-top way, which looked so funny, knowing what a tomboy she is. We must have seemed like a really weird little group standing in the middle of the main lane that runs through the Silver Spires grounds.

"Okay, I'll take you all!" I said, sighing a bit and pretending they were a lot of pestering children that I had to keep quiet somehow.

When they'd finished being amused by me for the second time in two minutes, Izzy started doing vigorous star jumps. "How come you don't feel the cold, Emily?"

"I'm just used to it, I suppose," I told her with a shrug. Then I looked at my watch. "Surely a few of the guests should have arrived by now, shouldn't they?"

Well that sent Izzy and Sasha straight back into their big excitement zone. "I can't wait to see them. I've got so many questions!" said Sasha.

"Me too!" squeaked Izzy. "And I bet they've got loads to ask each other, too. I mean, it'll seem so strange meeting up for a grand reunion party after all these years."

And then Nicole and Antonia were joining in with the buzz, while Bryony and I stood quietly to one side. Neither of us was looking forward to the afternoon in quite the same way as our friends were, and we'd only really come outside to look out for the guests arriving because the others had wanted us to.

"I suppose it'll be quite interesting when we get talking to people, but I'm not as excited as the others, are you?" I asked Bryony quietly.

She's a very thoughtful person, my best friend, so she didn't answer me straight away. But then her face suddenly brightened. "I'm looking forward to the tea!"

"Me too!" I said, giggling. "All those totally fab home-made cakes and biscuits!"

"I hope they decorate the hall to make it very grand," said Antonia, joining in with us now. "And use Silver Spires's best silver teapots and china!" she added, with a dreamy look in her eyes.

"Is that what your dad would do in his restaurant in Italy?" I asked her, because I'm interested in how the different countries all have their own traditions and ways of doing things.

"Afternoon tea isn't a custom in Italy, like it is in England," Antonia replied. "But yes, it's true, Papà makes his restaurant look extra-specially wonderful for important occasions."

Just about every time Antonia speaks I think how much her English has improved. When she joined Silver Spires with all the rest of us Year Sevens last September, she had trouble with lots of English words and she had a really strong Italian accent. But now you only notice her accent a bit. Nicole, her best friend, has helped her loads with the language. Antonia's also taught Nicole quite a bit of Italian, which Nicole has picked up really quickly, as she's the brainiest one in our group.

When Antonia started talking about decorations, I'd been imagining the big hall here in the beautiful old main building of Silver Spires full of women in their sixties all enjoying their grand reunion, introducing themselves to each other and chatting away about what they'd done since they'd left Silver Spires all those years ago. Now I suddenly felt myself wanting to break into giggles again.

"Isn't it funny the way everyone always calls them old girls?" I spluttered. "I mean it sounds kind of rude, doesn't it, to say, 'A load of old girls are coming to a reunion party at Silver Spires'!"

"Well, if you put it like that it sounds rude. But that's exactly what they are, aren't they?" said Nicole. "Old girls. It's really amazing that they're all coming back to meet up after fifty years."

"Yes, they might not even recognize each other," said Sasha. "It'll be so weird for them all, won't it? They'll be comparing notes about what boarding houses they were in and what their housemistresses were like..."

"Just think," I said, as something suddenly dawned on me, "this party could be *us* in fifty years' time."

"Yes," said Antonia, nodding firmly. "And we will all agree that it is Forest Ash which is the best boarding house, and Mrs. Pridham the best housemistress!"

"And Miss Stevenson the best assistant housemistress, and Miss Callow the best matron," I added.

"I've just had a thought!" said Nicole, looking shocked. "Forest Ash wouldn't have even existed fifty years ago, because it's one of the modern boarding houses, isn't it?"

Bryony was staring round. "That's right. In fact

the whole school must have been so much smaller in those days."

"I can't believe that we're just about the only Year Sevens who've signed up to come to the tea party," said Izzy, frowning. "It'll be really interesting talking to the –" she let out a giggle – "old girls!"

"See!" I said, stabbing my finger in the air with triumph, which was a bit over-the-top, I have to admit. "It *is* funny!"

"Yes, but seriously," Izzy carried on, "don't you think it'll be great to ask them questions about the old days and what the rules were like and the uniform and whether they had midnight feasts..."

"And what the lessons were like," Nicole chimed in.

"Yes, and what kind of things they got up to at weekends," said Izzy.

"And whether any of them came from foreign countries, and if they were homesick," Antonia added, looking a bit sad.

Nicole immediately put her arm round Antonia. "Imagine what it was like with no mobiles to call their parents or text them."

"And no e-mails," said Bryony. "Not even computers."

"What about TV?" asked Sasha. And we all

looked at Nicole for the answer to that one.

"Oh, they definitely had TV," she said, nodding. "Only it would have been black and white, I think."

Izzy's eyes shone. "I bet that not one single person who comes for the reunion today ever, *ever* imagined fifty years ago that they'd be coming back to Silver Spires fifty years later and their whole reunion would be filmed for TV. How amazing is that?"

"The TV crew will have set up the cameras by now, won't they?" said Sasha.

Izzy grabbed hold of Sasha's arms excitedly and spoke in one of her squeaks. "And then the cameras will be around school for another two weeks! It's going to be so exciting!"

Bryony tipped her head to one side and looked at Izzy. "We're supposed to act normally, remember?" she said, keeping her face straight.

"I know," said Izzy, immediately letting go of Sasha and straightening out her expression until she looked completely serious. "And I shall." She flicked her eyes across to Bryony. "Act normally," she added.

We all laughed, because Izzy looked anything *but* normal – in fact, she was practically going cross-eyed with the effort of not smiling.

"Look, here comes Juliet and her fan club,"
Bryony said. She rolled her eyes. "Looks like she
wants to be noticed by the cameras. What a
surprise."

I had to agree. We'd all been told to wear school
uniform this afternoon, even though it was a
Saturday, and whereas Juliet's friends looked pretty
normal, Juliet herself had a pair of high wedges on
and she'd rolled her school skirt over at the waist.
She'd also got loads of make-up on, so she looked
like a tall thin doll, in my opinion. I only know her
through riding club, but we don't get on at all
because I can't stand the way she's always showing
off during the hacks. Then afterwards she never puts
her saddle back on the saddle rack properly and
hardly ever bothers to wipe down the rest of the
tack. One time, when I saw her friend tidying up
after her, I gave them both a withering look, and
Juliet called me a little goody-goody.

"You're supposed to call her Jet, remember," said
Antonia, dropping her voice as Juliet approached.

It's true that absolutely nobody uses her proper
name, Juliet, because Juliet has told everyone to call
her Jet, which personally I think would be much
better suited to a pony. And whenever I hear
someone saying "Jet", I always want to break into

giggles as I imagine her neighing. She doesn't look anything like a pony though. In fact, she looks more like a model, with her nearly black hair that hangs exactly where it ought to hang, unlike my own bright auburn mop that lies in clumps and pokes out of the sturdiest hairband. Juliet is always going on about her hair being jet black, and then she bats her eyelashes and says, "It's such a coincidence that my name matches my hair!"

"Hey, guys!" she said, as she passed us. "Looking out for the visitors, are we? Ah, how sweet!" Then I caught her rolling her eyes at her friends, and I definitely heard a few sniggers before they walked on.

It really annoys me how Juliet always makes me feel so young and kind of pathetic, even though she's actually only one year older than us. Just then I found her extra annoying, because I was sure Bryony was right about the cameras, and Juliet wanted to be quite certain that, with her make-up and high shoes, she got plenty of attention.

I know it makes me the odd one out, but I wasn't all that excited when Ms. Carmichael, the headmistress, announced in assembly that Silver Spires was to be the subject of a TV documentary. You see, my family doesn't actually have a television

14

back home in Ireland – we've never had one, so I don't miss it. When I was at primary school and the other kids started talking about TV programmes, I just used to tune out. Sometimes they'd say, "Hey, Emily, isn't it weird not having a telly?" and they'd look at me as though I was a complete freak, but I didn't care. Things like that don't bother me. I asked them if it was weird not having horses to ride and cows to milk and chickens and rabbits to feed and vegetables to look after and eggs to collect. I think they probably thought I was even weirder after that little speech, but it still didn't worry me.

Actually there was one time I can remember when we were in the playground and everyone was talking excitedly about a programme they'd watched the evening before, and a girl asked me what I'd been doing instead of watching the programme. I can distinctly remember the pitying looks that everyone was giving me at that moment. But then the pity quickly changed to big respect when I told them I'd been helping Dad deliver a calf.

Now that I'm at boarding school, my life during term time is totally different from my life in the holidays. When I first came to Silver Spires last September, I felt like a fish out of water. It's true that Antonia had had further to come than me because of her family living in Italy, which is much further away than Ireland, and also it must have been terrible for Antonia not speaking much English. But for me it felt as though someone had drawn the curtains on my normal world and I had to learn how to live a different life.

At home I'm so free. Our farm is enormous, with loads of fields. We've got a proper big flower garden as well, and even better than that, a kitchen garden, as Mum calls it, with vegetables and herbs in it. I can spend all day in that garden, and it's not just planting and watering that I enjoy, it's the hard work as well – hoeing and raking and turning over the soil, and digging in the fertilizer to prepare it for planting. It's so satisfying making the soil tidy and rich, pulling out every single weed.

In the fields we've got a huge herd of cows and quite a few bullocks. And because the cows need milking every morning and evening, and Mum and Dad like to keep an eye on things, we've hardly ever been on holiday as a family. But I don't mind. I love my life, because it's the only one I've ever known... until I came here to Silver Spires.

I used to want to break out of the room where we have to do prep (that's homework, by the way) because the school days at Silver Spires are much longer than they were at primary and I'm always exhausted after all those lessons. It's not the lessons themselves that make me tired, it's just being inside all the time. Even now it's January and quite cold, I often feel like being outside, while the others are only up for watching something on TV.

I used to imagine how great it would be to lift my lovely farm life up from Ireland and drop it into Silver Spires, but now I'm used to it here, I feel totally happy that I've got the best of both worlds. Although, I do miss my gardening. When I first told the others that, they looked at me as though I was completely mad. It's hard to explain why I love it so much, but I always have done, ever since I was a little girl.

The grounds are absolutely massive at Silver Spires. They mainly consist of sports fields and lawns, as well as some grassy areas near Pets' Place, which is where a few girls keep their guinea pigs and rabbits and things that they've brought from home. Then there are the two massive shrubberies, one on either side of the lane where you first drive in, a few other shrubberies dotted about and two beautiful flower gardens. But that's all. No vegetable gardens.

And that's what I miss – the thrill of digging for potatoes. It feels like you're digging for gold.

And then you get the extra treat of eating all the vegetables, because they taste a million times better when you've grown them yourself. It's such a shame that at Silver Spires the vegetables are all bought into the school in big catering packs.

Anyway, I had to stop thinking about that. After all, there wasn't going to be anything pre-packed about today's special afternoon tea. Mrs. Pridham had told us there'd be chocolate eclairs, which are my personal favourite cakes ever, and all sorts of other delicious cakey things as well.

"Look! Look!" squeaked Sasha. "A car!"

"It's starting! The guests are arriving!" Izzy joined in excitedly.

"They might think we're the reception party if we stay here," said Bryony.

Izzy giggled. "A few Year Sevens shivering in the lane? I don't think so!"

"Anyway," said Nicole, "now we've caught a glimpse of them, let's go back to Forest Ash. We'll see them all properly at the party once they've had their welcome meeting with Ms. Carmichael and the Year Elevens."

We all agreed and started to walk away, but suddenly I couldn't resist looking back and saw two more cars coming along the lane. The second one was moving very slowly and, as it drew level with us, I noticed that the lady driving it was leaning forwards, flicking her head from side to side, staring out first to one side, then the other. On her face I caught such a look of wonder that I stopped in my tracks and tried to see the school through her eyes for a moment. It must have felt so strange to be seeing it after all those years.

Then the sun came out, blinding me for a moment, and at the same time Nicole broke my little spell, calling out, "Ems, come on! Sun's out!"

Nicole and Antonia have this kind of ritual where every time they go anywhere near the main school building when the sun is out, they stop and look at the silver spires. The whole building is really interesting to look at because it's so old and dark, with little diamond-shaped window panes and turrets and towers and a massive front door made of oak, which must weigh a ton. But the best thing about it is the way the sun shines on the tall spires so they gleam like silver, which is why the school is called Silver Spires. Even a watery sun will do it, which is what there was right now.

I went to catch up with them, but then hung back a bit and stared up at the beautiful spires, and wondered whether we were the first generation of

Silver Spires girls to do this, or whether generations and generations of girls had done it for the last fifty years. I would ask one of the guests that question. Yes, that's what I'd do.

And suddenly the thought of the party seemed a bit more interesting and exciting than it had done a few minutes before.

Chapter Two

It was weird to think that the party was taking place in the very same hall where Ms. Carmichael, the Head of the whole school, had made her announcement about the TV documentary. It looked so different now to when we were all crowded into it for that assembly. I'll never forget the gasp that went up with her first words: "I have been approached by a television production company who want to film our grand reunion, then stay on for a fortnight to film everyday life at the school."

It was actually halfway between a gasp and a "Yesss!" and it was followed by a deep silence.

because everyone wanted to hear more. Ms. Carmichael had gone on to explain that she didn't want our "happy, working lives", as she put it, to be disrupted in any way, and she'd also said we should just try to ignore the cameras if they happened to be around, and that soon we'd probably forget all about them anyway.

And now, this very same hall was full to bursting with women and bright lights, and loud talking and laughter and exclaiming, and the chink of teacups and glasses. There were a few men too, who must have been the husbands or people from the TV crew. It really was a totally brilliant atmosphere, and I felt perfectly happy standing beside one of the buffet tables with Bryony. Our other four friends were somewhere in the crowd, chatting away happily, but Bryony and I felt a bit awkward about just diving in and introducing ourselves.

"Look at Jet!" said Bryony.

I didn't need to follow Bryony's gaze to find where Juliet was. For a start you could hear her voice (and her silly whinnying laugh) standing out above all the noise. But she'd also placed herself as close as possible to one of the cameras, and I noticed she kept on glancing around and running her fingers through her hair while the two ladies she was supposed to be talking to chatted away with each other.

"I've counted over eighty guests." Bryony changed the subject. "About fifty old girls and thirty men."

"Had we better talk to someone?" I asked her, beginning to feel a bit self-conscious. It would be embarrassing if Bryony and I were the only spare-looking people in the whole room when it came to watching the finished film.

Bryony suddenly sounded very positive. "Yes, you're right. Let's go for it! Actually," she added, "I've just spotted an interesting-looking lady with really short hair like mine, only hers is grey."

And with that, she went plunging into the middle of the crowds and I was left standing on my own by the chocolate eclairs. Of course, being me, I couldn't resist taking another one. It was my third actually, but they were the scrummiest things I'd tasted in a long time.

As I munched away, I spotted Izzy and Sasha talking with a group of four ladies who kept on making big sweeping gestures with their hands. I wondered what they were trying to describe, but whatever it was, Izzy and Sasha looked genuinely interested. I wished I could get absorbed in a conversation with someone like that. The only two people I'd talked to so far had been going on about their grandchildren, which I actually found quite boring.

It took me a few seconds to spot Nicole and Antonia in a group with some Year Tens and an elderly couple. The woman was wearing the biggest smile and pointing up at the massive banner that the school had hung right across the width of the hall. In magnificent bright blue and silver lettering it said, *FIFTY YEARS ON: WELCOME, SILVER SPIRES OLD GIRLS*. And it was true, all the guests were being made very welcome.

I sighed as I swallowed the last bit of chocolate eclair and gulped down some orange juice. I really must make one last effort to talk to someone, or one of the teachers might come over and throw me out for only being there for the food.

Maybe I should do what Bryony did, and try to spot a lady with similar hair to mine. That was as good a way as any of picking someone to talk to. I looked round carefully and after a minute I was ready to give up, because *obviously* no one had a thick mass of wavy auburn hair tied back roughly into a hairband. But then I got a shock, because as a group of women moved towards one of the buffet tables, they left a bit of a gap in the room and I suddenly spotted a woman with auburn hair standing by the far window, staring outside. Her hair was miles neater and straighter than mine, but just the auburn colour was good enough for me. And even better, she seemed to be all on her own.

Once I've made up my mind to do something I always want to get on with it straight away, so I went zooming across that hall at a hundred miles an hour and nearly crashed into the poor lady when I reached the window.

"Hello, my name's Emily Dowd, I'm in Year Seven," I gabbled, giving her my best smile as I held out my hand.

The lady's eyes really sparkled as she shook my hand, and I was surprised because I was expecting a gentle handshake and yet she'd got a really strong grip. It must have shown on my face that she'd squeezed a bit too hard, because the sparkle was suddenly replaced by a look of horror. "Oh my goodness, I'm so sorry. I'm always doing that!" she said, clapping her hand to her mouth. "My husband used to tell me I ought to cool it a bit or I'd make people faint! Anyway it's nice to see you again."

I couldn't help laughing. The lady sounded practically like someone of my own age. But I was a bit confused. What did she mean when she said "again"?

"My name is Emily Peters," she went on, then she glanced at my hair and nodded. "So that's *two* things we have in common."

I felt my heart beating faster but I wasn't sure why. Maybe it was just the coincidence. Or maybe it was because suddenly I didn't feel bored any more. I was actually enjoying the thought of finding out all about this other Emily. Only there was one problem – I wasn't sure if I should be calling her "Emily" or "Mrs. Peters".

"My nickname is Ems," I said, hoping that she might give me a clue about what I was supposed to call *her*.

But she didn't. She just smiled again and said, "Ems, that's nice."

"Er…have we met before?"

She frowned as though she didn't know what I was talking about, but then she broke into a kind of knowing smile. "You're the girl I saw when I was driving in, aren't you?"

That gave me another surprise. Emily Peters was so observant. I couldn't believe that she'd recognized me, though I expect I might have recognized her too if I'd not had the sun in my eyes earlier. I suddenly wanted to find out what she thought about the silver spires, but she might have thought

I was a bit weird if I came out with such a question straight away. So I asked her something a bit more normal instead. "Er…which year were you in fifty years ago?"

"I understand from Ms. Carmichael that it's called Year Nine," she replied, her eyes flickering towards the window. "Only we didn't call it Year Nine back then. We called it Upper Fourth."

I wondered if she was already a bit bored with me, because she seemed more interested in something outside. Yet when I looked out myself, there was nothing to see.

"Oh, sorry, Ems," she suddenly said, leaning forwards and looking at me properly. "I'm so rude, aren't I?" Then she laughed. "Fancy having to apologize twice in such a short time. I was just looking at the grounds." She sighed a sort of satisfied sigh. "I can't wait for the guided tour. There's something I particularly want to see."

"Really? What's that?" She'd definitely got me curious now. "*I* could be your guide if you want," I said impulsively.

Her eyes seemed to be boring into mine as though she was trying to work out whether I'd made a bad suggestion or a good one, but then she slowly shook her head.

"Don't worry. I ought to wait for the official tour, I suppose. It's just that I used to run a gardening club. That's probably the memory that stands out the most for me from my time here. And I badly want to see if the vegetable garden's still here."

I gasped. "Oh! Wow!" She'd really given me a shock with those words. A lovely one. But a bit of a scary one too, because that made *three* things we had in common. I was just about to point that out when I suddenly realized how disappointed she was going to be when she actually went on the tour.

I had to warn her. "Oh dear," I said quietly. "There isn't a vegetable garden here now."

Her face seemed to cloud over. "Really? Well that's not good news."

"Sorry..."

"No, don't be sorry." She sighed again, but this time it was a sorrowful one. "It's probably better that you mentioned it. I'd hate to go round the back of the kitchens and find out for myself."

My heart was racing because I hadn't thought of there being a garden behind the kitchens. "Well, I've never actually...been there."

"Is it out of bounds?"

"I don't know. We just...never go round there. So that's where you had your gardening club?" I wanted to know as much as possible about what it had been like. "And what kind of things did you grow?"

I was expecting her to just mention a couple of vegetables, so it was a lovely surprise when she said, "Oh, all sorts. Potatoes, carrots, cucumbers, beans, lettuces, onions, turnips, leeks. The usual stuff."

It was absolutely incredible. Fifty years ago Emily Peters had been in charge of a gardening club, and now here was I, the keenest gardener in the world, talking to her.

"How many people were in your club?" I asked, wanting to build up a picture of what it might have been like.

"About twenty of us. We took turns to look after the plants. But I loved it so much, I was out there every free moment I had, whether it was my turn or not."

"And have you met anyone here today who was in your club back then?"

She shook her head. "Well...yes, a couple of people, but they seem to have forgotten how good it was... Or maybe I was under some massive illusion when I was in the Upper Fourth. Maybe I was the only one enjoying it and the others were all doing it under sufferance." She suddenly laughed a dry little laugh. "Anyway, I know you young folk aren't into things like gardening, so I'll shut up about it and change the subject now."

"No!" I said. But it must have come out a bit abruptly, because Emily's eyes widened and she took a step back.

"Sorry…I mean, please don't stop talking about it," I quickly said. "It's one of my favourite subjects. My family's got a farm in Ireland, you see, and when I lived at home all the time I was in charge of our kitchen garden, so I'm used to growing my own vegetables."

Her whole face seemed to light up when I said that. "Really?"

"Yes, and I so wish there was a vegetable garden at school. I've been wishing that ever since I've been here. You can ask my friends."

She took another step back and I realized that I must have been a bit loud. "Sorry…"

She laughed. "I believe you, it's okay! And we really must stop apologizing to each other!" Then she leaned forwards and the sparkle was back in her eyes. "Tell you what, I think I'd like to take you up on that offer of yours. Let's go and explore behind the kitchens!"

I nodded, feeling excited, and glanced across the room to see where Bryony was. I spotted her almost immediately, sitting down with a man with a walking stick. She was listening intently to whatever he was saying so I decided to just go. After all, I'd be back in no time and she probably wouldn't even miss me.

It was as we were crossing the big reception hall, making our way to the front door that we both turned to see a man with a camera on his shoulder hurrying after us.

Juliet was right behind him. "Emily, what's up? Anything I can help with?" she asked, as though she was my best friend all of a sudden.

It made me cross, because she was darting in front of the camera as she spoke and it was obvious she only wanted to draw attention to herself. She didn't really care about what we were doing.

"We're fine, thanks," I told her firmly.

She'd caught up with us in a flash, though, and was walking alongside Emily. "Hello," she said, smiling away. "My name's Jet Playden-Smythe. I'm in Year Eight, so I might know my way around better than Emily."

My blood boiled at that moment, and I wished Juliet would just go away and stop bugging me.

"I'm Emily Peters," said Emily, and I knew it was

horrible of me, but I really hoped she'd give Juliet one of those killer handshakes she'd given me. As it happened, though, she didn't shake her hand at all. Just kept right on walking, with me beside her.

"Er...it's the guided tour soon," Juliet said, rushing ahead of us to open the front door.

"Yes, I'll be back for that," said Emily, nodding firmly.

"See you," I said casually to Juliet as we went out and left her holding the door open for the cameraman to follow us.

She gave me such an evil stare at that moment, and I knew she hated the fact that I hadn't told her where Emily and I were going, and that the camera was following us and not paying any attention to her.

"My goodness, this hedge has grown!" said Emily. She was walking quite quickly and I was feeling more and more excited with every step, because there was a chance that I might be about to set eyes on the most wonderful garden and then I could ask if I could help look after it, and my life at Silver Spires would be truly complete.

"Oh, this fence is new," Emily went on. Her

footsteps were quickening and her eyes were bright. "Right, through this gate here and…"

My heart pounded.

"…and then…we should find… Oh!"

She stopped abruptly, but I hadn't missed the horror in her voice. We were staring at a big piece of land, overgrown with tangled weeds and nettles and brambles and grasses, the rest of the earth bare and hard. There was a large brick building ahead of us, with air extractors in the windows. So this was what the back of the kitchens looked like. It was very quiet and peaceful. I couldn't even hear any kitchen-type noises, only birds singing and a few distant girls' voices drifting on the air.

I bent down and felt the earth, then turned to look at Emily. It was as though she was rooted to the spot.

"This is so sad," she said quietly, shaking her head.

I felt sorry for Emily and didn't know what to say. If I asked her how the garden used to look, would it make her even sadder? I decided to risk it as I was dying to know, but I spoke quietly, because somehow that seemed a bit kinder.

"Er…was the garden ever bare, or did you have something growing all the year round?"

Emily kept staring straight ahead of her, and I guessed she was visualizing the garden as it used to be. "More or less, yes." Then she did a little laugh. "We had the old school favourites, like swede and spinach and carrots. Not *our* favourites, mind you. No, us girls preferred peas and broad beans, even though we only got to eat them at the end of the summer term and the start of the autumn term."

"I love broad beans," I said, but I'm not sure if Emily heard me. Her face had suddenly come alive.

"There was always great excitement as Halloween drew near..."

"Oh, you grew pumpkins!" I said, clapping my hands together like a little girl.

Emily laughed. Her eyes were really dancing and I was so pleased she'd lost that sad look completely. "Well, not quite. We used to carve mangolds, which are like big swedes, back then. And we had competitions to see who could grow the biggest one. Do you know, I never won!"

I didn't want Emily to lose the twinkle in her eye, but already she seemed to be getting sad again, because she sighed deeply and slowly.

"And did you have a compost heap?" I quickly asked, then realized that could seem a bit of an odd question.

"Yes we did."

"So you recycled all the peelings and everything? That's what we do at home, and it's how it ought to be everywhere, I think."

Emily turned and looked at me carefully when I said that. "You really are a gardener, aren't you?"

A little glow of pride seemed to shine inside me and I bent down to feel the earth, to cover the pinkness that was spreading up my cheeks.

"It's good soil underneath," said Emily.

I nodded as I straightened up. "I've been so wanting the chance to do some gardening and this plot would be the perfect place."

Then I took a proper look around. There was a large house off to my left behind a wall. It was built of dark red brick, with ivy clinging to it. The green and the red looked beautiful together and I wished I had my camera with me so I could take a photo and send it to Mum. She loves things like that.

"That's the headmistress's house," said Emily.

I gasped, then felt stupid because there was so much I didn't know about Silver Spires, and it seemed ridiculous that someone who was here fifty years before was having to tell me about the place. Then I had another surprise, because an old man was approaching us from a gap in the hedge that separated Ms. Carmichael's house from this plot of land. He looked as if he was in his sixties and for a second I thought he was one of the guests, but then I realized he couldn't be, not wearing overalls and big boots.

"Hello there! Can I help you?" he said.

"I…we…were just looking around."

Emily was staring at the old man, her eyes narrowed, and I felt even more stupid for not knowing who he was, as I couldn't introduce Emily to him.

"We just came along to look at the old garden," she was saying. "Well, it's not a garden now. I guess it's had its heyday."

"Right," said the man, his crinkly face breaking into a smile. "You must be one of the old girls?"

"Yes, I'm Emily Peters."

"Emily?" repeated the man, frowning.

They were shaking hands and I could see the look in Emily's eyes changing. Her eyes weren't narrow and staring any more, but wide and bright. "Don't tell me it's Stanley?"

Stanley nodded. "Stan. Yes. But I'm afraid I don't remember an Emily Peters."

Emily smiled. "Peters is my married name. I used to be Emily Harrington."

Stan took a step backwards as though the shock had made him lose his balance. "Emmy Harrington! Well I never!" he said. And I saw that his eyes were shining with tears.

"You're still working here, Stan. I can't believe it!" Emily's voice was soft and a bit shaky.

I looked from one to the other of them and then noticed that the cameraman was filming away just inside the gate. And I thought how lucky he was, like me, to be here witnessing this very special moment in time.

Chapter Three

It was unbelievable that Emily and Stan used to know each other fifty years ago, and that Stan was still here at Silver Spires. When they'd both recovered from their shock, Emily introduced me to Stan, then asked him why he hadn't been at the reunion.

"I was invited to come along," he replied. "But I thought I might feel a bit out of place just being the old gardener, so..."

His voice faded out, and he kicked the earth with his boot. "Nothing growing here any more." He pointed to the far end of the plot, nearest the kitchen.

"Even the old herb garden's gone to seed."

"So there...used to be...things growing all over this plot?" I asked, feeling a bit unsure about whether I was interrupting.

It was Emily who answered. "You wouldn't believe it from seeing it now, Ems, but this was such a fine vegetable garden once upon a time, with all its broad beans, runner beans, broccoli..."

"Brussels," put in Stan. "And cabbage, carrots... spuds."

"Leeks," added Emily. Then she laughed. "You name it, we grew it. Isn't that right, Stan?"

"Yep...those were the days."

"Yes...those were the days," repeated Emily in a whisper that faded into silence as they both stared at the plot.

"I'm going to get those days back again," I said, almost to myself, feeling a big determination zapping right through my whole body as a picture of how the garden must have looked started to take shape in my imagination.

Stan looked up sharply and I could see I'd caught his interest. "The thing is, young Emily, it was the way of the world in those days," he explained. "After the war, there wasn't as much food to go around. It was rationed for years and so we got used to being self-sufficient. That's why we grew our own vegetables here. There was no other way of doing things. But then the school got bigger and the country grew more prosperous and bit by bit they started modernizing things and bringing in catering packs of this and that. Broke my heart, to be honest."

"So did the garden just…get left?" I asked, feeling some of Stan's and Emily's sadness rubbing off on me.

"It was a gradual thing," said Stan. "But the final decision to stop using it to grow veggies came two headmistresses before this one."

"That must have been after Miss Telford. She was the Head when I was here," said Emily.

"That's right," Stan said, nodding. "I was the under gardener then. There were just the three of us, who worked all hours." He looked around and didn't speak for a few seconds and I got the feeling he was really sad. "Mind you, the place didn't look like it does now. I mean, Silver Spires has grown bigger and bigger over the years. So now there are groundsmen, rather than gardeners. They do a fine job tending the shrubberies and mowing the lawns, keeping the sports fields in order, fencing and trellising, looking after the buildings – you name it…" Stan nodded slowly and turned to Emily. "I just keep up Ms.

Carmichael's garden and do a few odd jobs around her house now. It's not the same as the good old days at all." He stopped and looked around again.

I felt sorry for Stan. And in my mind an idea had been gradually forming as he'd been talking, which was starting to fill me with big excitement. I was imagining how cool it would be if things really did go back to how they were, with all the vegetables we ate at mealtimes being grown right here in this garden. But the best bit of my idea was that I could actually start a gardening club, just like Emily's but fifty years later. The moment the thought had hit me, I wished I could find out straight away if I was allowed, as I knew I'd have to get permission first. Maybe I'd just see whether Stan thought it was a good idea, though.

"Do you think I'd be able to start up a gardening club here, Stan? If we worked hard and cleared this whole plot, I mean?"

"Not up to me, I'm afraid." He laughed a funny dry little laugh that made me sad again. "I'm on my way out. Just about to retire. You'd need to ask Tony that one. He's in charge – Site Manager, that's his official title." He kicked the ground again with his sturdy old boot so the top layers of soil broke, then he heaved a sigh. "Although, thinking about it,

Tony's only taking orders from other folk. I should ask your boarding housemistress. Yes, that'd be the best thing." His face suddenly brightened. "Tell you what, though, I've got an old photo or two somewhere if you're interested to see how that garden used to be. I'll rootle them out for you if you like."

"Yes, I'd love to see the photos... Thank you."

"Actually I'd be very interested to see them myself," said Emily. "Maybe you could post me one if I gave you my address? I'd make a copy, of course, and send it straight back," she added.

"The guided tour is just about to begin!"

The camera that I now realized had still been on us swung round at the sound of Juliet's loud voice coming from the other side of the gate. And it felt as though a magic spell had been broken at that moment.

"Right you are," called Emily. "We'll be straight over."

Juliet smiled at the camera and ran her fingers through her hair, then turned and walked away. I don't know why that annoyed me so much. But it did. It was funny though...even with all that irritation going on inside my head, nothing could spoil the excitement I felt. All I wanted to do was run back to

Bryony and the others and tell them what a brilliant time I'd been having, and then go straight to Mrs. Pridham to ask her about starting up a gardening club. But then I suddenly remembered the other important thing.

"Er, when could I look at the photos?" I asked Stan.

"Let me see...Tuesday. I'll bring them to school with me. How's that suit you?"

I nodded hard. "Thank you."

Emily had pulled some cards out of her handbag. She handed one to Stan and one to me. "That's my address. And I'd love to hear how you're getting on with the garden from time to time. I can't tell you how happy I am that you want to start a gardening club again."

"Yes, yes. I'll let you know. I can't wait!"

"Good for you, Ems! Good for you!"

And my heart squeezed with pride. But it wasn't only pride. There was something else too. Ambition, that's what it was.

Yes, ambition

It was very early on Sunday morning and the six of us were in our dorm (which is called Emerald dorm, by the way. All the Year Seven dorms are named after precious stones and I was so pleased when I first found out I was in Emerald, because of coming from Ireland, which is sometimes called the Emerald Isle). I'd dragged everyone out of their beds and we were all crammed onto mine for a truth talk. It was Antonia who first came out with the name "truth talk", because that was her funny Italian way of describing the kind of conversation you have when you're confiding in your friends. Any one of us can call a truth talk if we've got something specially important we want to discuss, and then the others all pile onto that person's bed. We'd already had one the day before because I'd had so much to tell everyone about Emily Peters and Stan and the garden and how it used to be with all the students working on it, and everyone eating the vegetables at mealtimes. And I'd explained that the land was in a terrible state now, but that if we got a gardening club started, we could dig up all the weeds, prepare the soil and get it ready for planting.

I can't say that my friends were exactly over the moon with my idea, but I knew I'd be able to bring them round to it once they realized what good fun gardening is. And actually they must have been looking forward to it quite a lot because they all seemed really pleased when Mrs. Pridham gave me permission to start the club. I love thinking back to what she actually said when I asked her about it that Saturday evening.

"I'm so pleased to hear that someone wants to do something green like this. And the headmistress approves too. Well done, Emily!" Then she'd told me that I'd have to ask Tony about what land I could use, as he was in charge of the grounds. She'd promised to have a word with him first, and I'd persuaded her to leave a message on his voicemail right then and there. I was hoping he'd get it before Monday because he's got a house on the premises and often works at weekends, so he might have been able to help us straight away.

Going over all that in my mind was what had made me want to call the truth talk now.

"Listen, guys," I began, as soon as everyone was settled on my bed. "I've been thinking about the gardening club... In fact, I've been dreaming about it all night long. And I'm going to see if I can find Tony straight after this, before breakfast even, to ask him about that plot of land behind the kitchens. Who wants to come with me?"

I smiled brightly round at my friends and then realized they were all still half asleep, looking at me blearily as though they couldn't take in what I was saying properly. Never mind, I knew they'd be all right in a few minutes.

"Is that what you dragged us out of bed to tell us?" asked Nicole through a big yawn.

"No," I quickly said. "Not just that. There's something else. You know how Ms. Carmichael has got a thing about recycling, with the banks she's set up for paper and plastic cups and stuff? Well, there's one big thing she's forgotten, and that's food! Think about it – there are three hundred and sixty girls in this school and just about every one of us has at least one piece of fruit a day, as well as all the vegetables in our school meals, and the peelings could be put on a big compost heap to mulch down into compost to put on the new vegetable plants, to grow even more. Ta-da!"

I paused to let my words sink in, because everyone still looked half asleep.

"Yes, that sounds really good," said Bryony eventually, as the others made kind of grunting noises.

I couldn't help feeling really disappointed that they weren't more interested, but it was probably just that they usually have a lie-in on Sundays and I'd kind of ruined that for this morning. I knew I'd been selfish, but I couldn't help it – I was so excited about my new project. I jumped off my bed and went to the bathroom to have a shower, then I rushed back to get dressed and found that everyone except Bryony had gone back to bed.

"I'll come with you," Bryony said.

I hugged her. "Thanks, Bry. You're a star!"

We walked along in silence because Bryony never speaks unless she's got something proper to say, and I simply didn't feel like talking because now that I was hopefully about to speak to Tony, I was getting scared. What if he said I couldn't have the land I wanted? It was no good having permission for a gardening club if there was nowhere to garden.

"I don't want anyone to know about the plans for the club, Bry," I began hesitantly. "Not until... I...definitely know it's all right to use the plot that Emily showed me."

"Let's hope those cameras don't follow us, then," said Bryony, which made me gasp.

"*What* cameras?"

But I didn't need to ask. I'd suddenly spotted them way up ahead near the swimming pool block. "Oh no! They're heading in this direction!"

"Doesn't matter," said Bryony in her usual unfazed way. "Just keep walking and if they ask us what we're doing, we're...taking exercise."

"Yes, good thinking, Bry." I was so lucky having Bryony as a best friend, because nothing ever bothers her.

As we drew nearer, though, we saw that we didn't have to worry. Juliet and two of her friends were walking briskly along towards us, all three of them with sports bags slung over their shoulders. And walking alongside of them, looking as though he was having a bit of trouble keeping up, was the same cameraman who'd followed me and Emily out of the party. I could hear Juliet laughing as she talked and I could tell she was loving the attention. That meant she'd probably be perfectly happy if Bryony and I just scuttled past and left her to the limelight.

"We've been swimming," she was saying. "Actually we often go for a swim before breakfast. It sets you up for the day."

"Sounds like she's acting in an advert," said Bryony under her breath. And I thought it looked it too, because Juliet's hair was completely dried and styled. When I go swimming, which is as little as possible, I always come out with my hair sticking out even more than it usually does and dripping down my back, making an uncomfortable wet patch just below my shoulders.

"So what time did you have to get up?" the man filming asked her.

She stopped and looked at her watch. "I guess about six thirty. I don't set my alarm clock, I just use my body clock."

"We're on our way to breakfast now," one of her friends added.

"Yes, swimming makes you starving hungry but the breakfasts at Silver Spires are yummy," said Juliet, sounding all bubbly and bright.

We were almost right up to her by then and for a moment I thought we might be able to sneak by without anyone even noticing us. But to my horror, when we drew level, the man suddenly swung his camera round so it was facing me and Bryony.

"Here's another couple of early birds," he said.

I'll never forget the thunderous look on Juliet's face. She stood rooted to the ground, hands on hips, as the cameraman carried on talking directly to me.

"No swimming bag, so I guess you're just taking a walk before breakfast?"

I nodded. "Yes…we're just…" I didn't know what else to say, but I had to say something. I didn't want to look stupid on the film. "…Taking a walk."

The moment I'd spoken I realized how pathetic I must have sounded repeating exactly what he'd said, and I wasn't the only one to think that either. Juliet and her friends were smirking as they watched me go red, and the cameraman swung round to catch their amusement, which made my blood boil and probably made me look redder than ever. But Bryony was walking on and I knew that was the most sensible thing to do, so I followed her, trying to ignore the rage that was flaring up inside me. And neither Juliet nor the cameraman said anything else, thank goodness.

We finally spotted Tony in the distance over near Pets' Place. None of my friends have got pets at school, so we don't often have any reason to come all the way over here.

"Tony! Tony!" I called in my big happiness at having found him.

"Ssh!" said Bryony.

It was true I was being far too loud. I'd only ever actually said the word "Hello" to Tony, and now I was acting as though he was my long-lost uncle or something.

We broke into a jog and as we got near to him

I noticed he looked really alarmed. "You all right, girls?"

"Yes, we're fine," said Bryony. "Emily's just excited because we've been looking for you for ages."

Tony looked relieved to hear that, and turned to me, eyebrows raised. My heart started hammering as the dread that I might not be able to have the plot of land I wanted came flooding back. Since my talk with Emily and Stan, I hadn't stopped thinking how happy they'd both be to see that land restored to its former glory.

"Er...well, you see, I'm starting a gardening club..."

"Yes, I got the message from Mrs. Pridham."

"...and I want to grow vegetables and—"

"Vegetables, eh? Well, I don't see why you shouldn't grow a few veggies. Look, there's a little patch right here."

He was striding off, heading even closer to Pets' Place. "Nice and handy to feed the pets, eh? A few carrots and that?" He was grinning at us over his shoulder and I hurried to catch him up.

"No, sorry. I really wanted a bigger plot of land..."

It was on the tip of my tongue to tell him my plans about changing Silver Spires back to how it used to be, growing its own vegetables. But then he might think I was just a silly little Year Seven with big ideas, and I'd never be able to explain that I was used to proper gardening and knew what I was talking about.

"What about that land behind the kitchens?" Bryony suddenly asked. "There used to be a vegetable garden there, didn't there?"

I felt myself tensing up as Tony stopped in his tracks and turned round. I kept my eyes glued to his face, searching for a change of expression, dreading him bursting out laughing and saying it was out of the question because that site was being used for something else entirely. But as it happened, he just tipped his head to one side as though he was considering it, and I dared to allow myself to hope.

"Maybe you could use the old herb garden patch," he said eventually.

"The herb garden? Is that part of the big garden?"

He nodded. "Yep. The kitchen staff kept it going until quite recently, but there's not really much point having a few home-grown herbs when the rest of the food is all supplied by outside firms."

"But why do the vegetables have to be bought in? Why can't the school grow its own vegetables?"

I asked, feeling suddenly daring, but still dreading the answer.

"You're joking!" said Tony. "There are three hundred and sixty girls to feed here. High-maintenance stuff is no good in a place like this."

He was looking at me as though I was mad, but Mum and Dad often talk about high and low maintenance and productivity, so I know a bit about it and I couldn't help coming right back at him for what he'd just said.

"The thing about growing your own vegetables and herbs is that it's only high maintenance if you let it slip."

He looked a bit startled for a moment, then broke into a grin. "Exactly! That's why it's high maintenance – because you *can't* let it slip, which takes manpower, and all our manpower is taken up looking after the grounds and the buildings."

But I couldn't stop arguing my case, even though I felt a bit rude, because I was so sure I was right. "If there was a gardening club, we'd have *loads* of manpower...only it would be girl power!"

"You'd need a pretty big gardening club to provide the whole of Silver Spires with vegetables!" Tony shook his head and pursed his lips. "And I know what you girls are like... You've got too many other things on the go to stick with something. Especially something like gardening."

I could feel my hackles rising but I could also feel Bryony's elbow in my side. She was telling me I shouldn't be arguing with Tony, and I knew she was right.

"Well, could we just have the herb patch for the gardening club, please?" I asked in a gabble.

"I think that would probably be okay." Tony looked at his watch and I felt myself panicking a bit. *Probably* wasn't good enough. I wanted *definitely*. Maybe if *I* started talking definitely and mentioned tools and things…

"Er, I'll need a spade and a hoe and a rake – you know, not the flimsy sort…"

He looked a bit taken aback, then nodded. "I can supply you with whatever you need, don't worry. Okay, tell you what, I'll see you at lunchtime tomorrow at the old herb garden. Do you know where to go?"

"Yes, I…I do."

"That's settled then."

"Tomorrow?" I didn't think I could wait that long.

"Thank you very much," said Bryony. "We'll be there after lunch."

"Yes, thank you, Tony," I added as Bryony grabbed my wrist and started dragging me away.

"Grown-ups always take ages to sort stuff out," she said, the moment we were out of earshot. "And just think – you've got yourself a gardening club to start, you've got yourself a plot of land, and all in less than forty-eight hours from when you first thought of it. So that's pretty good, isn't it?"

And when she put it like that, I had to agree it *was* pretty good.

Chapter Four

Lessons have never gone so slowly on a Monday morning as they are doing right now. I'm stuck here in ICT and Mrs. Lawson is going on and on about organization, storage and access, when all I want to do is meet Tony.

Actually, I think Mrs. Lawson might be getting a bit exasperated with me. "Emily, why are you continually looking out of the window this morning?"

Because I want to get digging and I'm scared it's going to rain.

"Sorry."

I tried hard to concentrate on that other window, the computer one on the screen in front of me, but five seconds later my eyes had strayed back to the real one. It was looking very overcast. I glanced up at the clock. Nearly time for the bell. Good. Then just lunch to get through before my big plan could be put into action. All my friends had said they'd come with me to the herb garden, to help me get started. I knew it wouldn't be a proper club with just my friends in it, but I had to start somewhere, and as yesterday had gone on, it had been lovely to hear them asking me more and more questions about what tools we'd be using and which vegetables could be grown at what times of year. And they also admitted that they'd been too tired to take in what I'd been saying before breakfast, but they were genuinely interested.

The moment the bell went, Bryony and I jumped up. She likes ICT about as much as I do, which is not at all. Izzy was next out of the block, because she's almost as bad as me at sitting still, but for a different reason. Mine is to do with wanting to be outside, but hers is because she's done ballet to a very high level and it doesn't feel right to her to be sitting around for long. She'd rather be stretching her muscles.

The others followed close behind and we all rushed over to the dining hall. The ICT block is a bit of a way from the main building, though, so by the time we got to the dining hall there was quite a queue and loads of people had started eating. In fact, some girls were already handing in their pudding plates. They must have got choir or sports practices to go to.

When we were at the counter I found myself taking a big interest in what the dinner ladies were doing with the leftover fruit peelings as they cleared the plates. I'd never paid attention to that before, but if we were to get back to proper gardening then we'd need really good compost, and nothing could be better than leftover peelings all mulched down.

I felt real prickles of disappointment when I saw one of the ladies tipping an apple core into a big rubbish bag that someone else had just scraped chicken bones into, and I couldn't help huffing a bit even though I knew I wasn't being fair on the dinner lady. You should never put meat into compost, but there was no reason why the food waste shouldn't be kept together at the moment. Once the gardening club got started, though, we could recycle it all properly. I couldn't wait.

"What's the matter?" asked Bryony, when we were sitting round a table together.

It always amazes me the way Bryony doesn't miss a thing. She'd even noticed that I was a bit irritated at the counter.

"Just seeing that dinner lady tipping an apple core in with old chicken leftovers," I said. "I know it's different here, but at home we always keep fruit and veg peelings for compost, and since I met Emily I can't stop thinking about how it used to be like that here too."

"Woo, listen to Little Miss Green!" came a familiar voice from just behind me.

I hadn't even realized Juliet was on the table next to us or I would have spoken a bit more quietly.

"Ignore her," mouthed Bryony.

But I couldn't help turning round and saying something, because she'd annoyed me so much. "It won't be long till the school starts recycling peelings and stuff for compost, actually."

"Oh really?" Her voice was so mocking I could feel myself starting to blush. "Emily's clearly been promoted to head of recycling at Silver Spires!" she added, which made a few of her friends snigger. Then she dropped her voice. "I bet she doesn't even know what recycling means."

"Ignore her," repeated Bryony, quietly but firmly.

But she was too late. The words were already

fighting to get out of my mouth, Juliet made me so mad. Of course I knew what recycling meant. "It's the cycle that happens over and over... That's what a cycle is. I mean, we make it happen because we recycle...like reusing stuff or..." The more I couldn't find the right words because of Juliet and her friends staring at me with their smirky expressions, the more I felt my hackles rising. And the sort of mocking but pitying look on Juliet's face was winding me right up. This was so unfair. I had to show her I wasn't completely stupid. "I might not be in charge of recycling, but I'm in charge of the new gardening club," I blurted out.

Then I wished I could shovel the words straight back in again, as Juliet started laughing loudly and, of course, all her friends followed suit.

I could feel myself blushing right to the roots of my hair. If only I'd taken Bryony's advice and just ignored Juliet. I carried on eating as though I wasn't bothered, but what she said next annoyed me even more.

"Some people are full of big ideas, but they've no idea what hard work it is to make them happen."

I was chewing away furiously so I could swallow my mouthful and get straight back at her. Only good old Bryony got in first.

She turned round and looked directly at Juliet, but didn't raise her voice or sound at all rattled. "Emily lives on a farm actually, *Jet*, and she's been gardening for years. So I should imagine she's got more understanding of hard work in her little finger than you've got in your whole body."

I thought that was a totally brilliant put-down, and so did my friends, because I noticed their eyes were all shining. *Jet*, however, was not impressed. She tossed her silky black hair and got up to go, her lips in a tight thin line. Immediately, her little crowd of fans got up too and off they marched. They hadn't even had their puddings. As soon as we six were on our own, every one of us burst into nervous giggles.

"Thanks for sticking up for me, Bry!" I said, hugging her.

She shrugged. "I was just telling the truth."

There was no sign of Tony when I went through the gate to my precious plot of land. But then I was a bit early, because I'd only had two mouthfuls of cheesecake for pudding, as I couldn't wait another second – I'd just had to get going. Bryony and the others had said they'd join me in a few minutes, and I was dying to show them the garden.

From where I was standing I thought I could tell which part of the plot Tony meant by the herb garden. It wasn't as overrun with weeds as the rest of the land and there were still quite a few plants in there, even though they were overgrown and dried up. That was a shame, because it's so easy to grow herbs. Mum grows them at home. We've got a little raised bed in the corner of the garden at the back of our farmhouse, with coriander, chives, mint and basil. Then we've got a window box with parsley and marigolds. Mum says the marigolds keep the bugs away.

I looked at the dull grey patch of land in front of me, and thought how brilliant it would be if it was full of bright herbs. Next I turned to survey the whole of the rest of the plot and imagined it with proper raised beds and a big compost heap in the corner. After that I got a bit carried away, picturing loads of students picking courgettes and runner beans and taking them into the kitchen.

"Hello there!" came a voice behind me, making me jump when I was right in the middle of my brilliant daydream. "You *are* keen, aren't you?"

It was Tony, and I nodded enthusiastically as he came to stand beside me, drumming his fingers on his arm and frowning at the straggly herbs.

"What a mess. I hope you don't mind hard work, because this ground needs a lot of preparing before anything can go in it. You do realize that, don't you?"

I was getting fed up with everyone going on about what hard work gardening is, and part of me felt like giving Tony a *duh* look and saying, *Of course I realize!* But I knew it was important to keep him on my side. Once I'd proved to him that I was good at gardening and I meant business, I would ask him if I could have the whole plot. But right now, I just needed lots of help so we could get this patch thoroughly dug and cleared of weeds and hoed and raked and ready for planting as soon as possible. That'd impress Tony.

"Yes, I know." I gave him my best smile and spoke in my politest voice. "Did you bring a spade? I want to get the ground prepared so I can plant some early potatoes in March."

Tony looked a bit startled, as though I'd asked him to bring a JCB to carve the land up. "You certainly know your mind, don't you? Are your parents gardeners?"

"No, they're farmers, but we grow all our own vegetables too."

"Ah!" He nodded and looked suddenly very

focused as he paced out an area of ground about five metres long and four metres wide, all around the old straggly herbs. He dug his heel in as he walked, to make a definite mark so we could see exactly where the boundary was. "There. I take my orders from the powers that be and that's how much land I've been told to give you for your gardening club. All right? Which means you could have a few potatoes, but not a lot else." He suddenly raised his eyebrows at me. "So you're used to working on the land?"

I didn't like the sound of "the powers that be". He couldn't have been talking about Mrs. Pridham, because Mrs. P had been the one to tell me to ask Tony. Tony must have had to ask someone else. I'd no idea who that could be. All I knew was that I badly wanted more land.

"It's only me and my friends at the moment, but once I've started a proper gardening club with lots of others, do you think we could have…some more?" I pointed in a vague kind of way at the rest of the land.

"No chance!"

It felt as though he'd just stamped on my toe.

"It's not up to me, mind," he went on in a softer tone as he walked round the boundary that he'd marked out, making it even clearer. Then he grinned.

"The powers that be reckon that this is enough for a gardening club, so I'm afraid that's your lot, okay?"

I wished I could tell him that no, it was not okay. I desperately wanted the whole garden, which was about ten times bigger. But I reminded myself that I had to be careful.

"Who...who exactly are the...powers that be?"

Tony laughed. "Domestic bursar." Then he started to walk back to the gate and I saw that he'd parked his pickup truck on the other side. "I've brought three spades, and a couple of hoes and rakes in the truck. Come and help me get them." I followed him, and on the way he turned round to point to a little outhouse at the far side of the kitchens. "See that door there? It's not locked and there's nothing in the outhouse. You can leave the tools in there when you've finished." He sighed and scratched his head as though he didn't know how on earth this gardening thing was going to happen. "You did say you'd got friends to help you, didn't you? Because this is going to be a long, slow job."

We'd reached his truck by then and I could see the tools, which gave me a little burst of excitement. "Yes, my friends are on their way."

And at that very moment they all appeared and

offered to help me carry everything over to the garden.

"Good timing!" said Tony. Then he tossed some gloves out of the front of the truck. "There you go! Only three pairs, mind. You'll have to go shopping for more if you're serious."

I'd already planned to ask Mrs. Pridham about that, but it annoyed me that Tony had added those last three words. Of course I was serious. He got in his truck then and started to pull away, still calling out to us. "Have fun! And don't worry if you change your mind. It's going to be hard work." His chuckle got mixed up with the sound of the truck's engine, before he shouted out one last thing: "Good job the matrons keep a nice supply of plasters, because I can tell you, you're going to get a few blisters!"

Then he was gone, and I was left fuming.

"What a cheek!" I hissed. "I never get blisters!" I marched back to the herb garden and leaned on my spade, eyeing the land. Then I suddenly realized the others were totally silent as they stood beside me, and when I looked at their faces I saw that their eyes were big and anxious. Apart from Bryony's.

"It's going to be great, Ems," she said, giving me a thumbs up.

"Don't take any notice of how it looks now," I told the others. "You won't believe how much you'll love it when it's all planted up. Honestly, it'll be all green and lovely!" They were still looking worried, though, so I kept chatting away. "I'll be meeting up with Stan tomorrow and he's going to show me some photos of how it used to be, remember!"

There was a silence, then Nicole shook her head slowly. "I wouldn't know where to start," she said quietly.

"I'll tell you what to do," I assured her brightly. "Look!" I bent down and tugged gently at a big weed, then pulled a bit harder, and felt a great thrill as it came out.

"But we can't start now!" said Antonia, looking shocked. "We'd get our uniforms and shoes completely messed up."

"And there are only three pairs of gloves," said Izzy. She spoke hesitantly. "The soil gets right under your nails, Ems."

Why was I the only one feeling excited? Even Bryony was frowning. And Sasha was looking at her watch.

"Actually, Ems, afternoon school's about to begin."

I felt a real stab of frustration when she said that. I'd no idea so much time had gone by since lunch, and I was desperate to make a start. "I'll be along in a sec," I said.

Sasha's eyes were wide. "You don't want to be late for Mr. Pattle, Ems. He *is* the strictest teacher at Silver Spires, remember. Can't you just wait till after school, when we're changed? Then we'll have loads of time."

"It's okay. You go. I'll just put the tools away. I'll catch you up."

So the others went off, calling out to me to hurry up. But the moment they'd gone, I went over to the corner of the herb garden and thrust the spade into the hard earth, then wriggled it further in with my foot. I heaved out a spadeful of soil, and – there! – I'd actually turned over my first bit of earth in my brand new garden. It felt brilliant and I couldn't help carrying straight on with the next and the next. It was so amazing, but I was a bit anxious, because it looked like Antonia was right – my shoes were already dirty and I'd got marks on my tights and skirt. Never mind, I'd probably be able to rub them off easily.

My eyes went back to the soil. Already you could see the dull grey turning black. I glanced at the sky and noticed happily that it wasn't quite so cloudy as it had been earlier. Good. That meant that I could come back after school and have a proper go. It felt wonderful to imagine how clean and soft and rich the land was going to be by the time I'd finished, and I so wished I could carry on all afternoon. But I knew it was time I ought to get going to face geography and the boring subject of maps and their scales with Mr. Pattle. I glanced at my watch and that's when I got a massive shock. Mr. Pattle's lesson would be just about finishing. I must have been in a total dream doing my gardening – I couldn't believe the time had gone so fast. I'd just have to make some excuse next time I saw him. I could say I'd been stuck in the loo feeling sick, but then I'd got better so it must have been something I'd eaten. Yes, that's what I'd say.

What was it after geography? French. Right. Luckily there are toilets and washbasins near the language labs, so I'd have time to get cleaned up and then I'd go straight into Madame Poulain's lesson.

I moved at a hundred miles an hour, putting away the tools, then racing out of the garden, trying to rub the soil off my hands.

Chapter Five

At the end of school I quickly got changed into my tracky bums and wellies and went rushing over to my new garden. I'd asked the others if they'd come along to help, but unfortunately they'd all realized they had other stuff to do. Nicole had swimming training for the gala, Bry had to go to a meeting about an Outward Bound course that she was interested in, and the others had clubs. I didn't mind, as they'd all promised to join me the next time. But I felt frustrated while I was jogging over, because I realized I'd only got about half an hour before it would be too dark to see.

I set to work quickly, digging with the spade, then breaking up the soil bit by bit with the hoe and dragging out the weeds and old roots, thinking how well everything had turned out earlier on. Bryony had said that when Mr. Pattle asked where I was, she didn't know what to say, so she'd mumbled something about a stomach ache and he'd been fine with that. Then I'd turned up, just about clean and tidy enough, in time for the beginning of French. And now here I was enjoying myself in my garden again. Even though I'd only done what seemed like a tiny patch, I'd done it really thoroughly and I was accumulating quite a pile of weeds and old plants to start a compost heap. It would be small but at least it would be a start.

Now, where would be the best place for it? I turned to look around, and that was when I realized one of the cameramen was standing there filming me.

"Sorry, didn't mean to startle you," he said. "You're certainly deep into the work, aren't you?"

I just nodded and went back to my hoeing, because I didn't feel like talking when I was trying to plan my garden.

"So is this like a project or something?" he asked, as I bent down to pull out more weeds.

"It's a...gardening club," I replied, feeling a bit of a fool because I was all on my own.

"Oh, right. How many people in the club?"

I tried not to blush. "It's only just started."

He didn't ask any more questions, but I was left feeling embarrassed about not seeming to have anyone at all in the club, and I decided to have a proper talk to the others later about getting more people to join. I'd kind of forgotten about that important point in my excitement over starting work in the garden. Maybe I could put up posters. That would be better than making an announcement in assembly, because it would mean I wouldn't have to put up with hearing Juliet sniggering about me with her friends. I remembered how she'd laughed at the idea of a gardening club and I thought she and all her friends would laugh even more if they saw the tiny plot of land I'd got. But I shouldn't think about that now. So I pulled my mind back to my pile of weeds... and felt a wave of hopelessness coming over me.

This was nothing like my proper plan. I wanted a great big compost heap in a great big garden with every single scrap of biodegradable waste from the whole school on it. It was just so frustrating that so much good stuff that could be recycled was being thrown away instead.

The cameraman had stopped filming me and gone, thank goodness, so I just stared at my tiny plot as Tony's words ran through my mind.

I take my orders from the powers that be...the domestic bursar.

I didn't even know who the domestic bursar was. In fact, come to think of it, I didn't even know what *domestic bursar* meant. But at that moment, I felt a sudden big determination to talk to him or her.

Yes, that's what I'd do. I'd get my proper plan into action.

The following lunchtime I was full of energy. Once again I was bolting my food so I could get out to my precious garden, because today was a really lovely day. The sun was shining and that made all six of us happy.

"If the sun is still shining after school then I will help in your garden, Emily," said Antonia, smiling.

"Me too," said Nicole. "And isn't this the day when Stan's going to show you his photos? I'm dying to see a picture of how it all looked fifty years ago."

"Ssh!" I said, looking round. "I don't want Juliet to hear us talking about the garden. She'll only take the mick."

"What is a mick?" asked Antonia, looking confused. "And why will Jet take it from you?"

It's so sweet when Antonia doesn't understand expressions that we all take for granted, and Nicole quickly explained, as she always does. Then Sasha pointed out that I had nothing to worry about, because Juliet was over the other side of the hall, at a table near the counter.

"And it's perfectly obvious why," said Izzy, rolling her eyes as she nodded at the cameraman who was standing only about a metre away from where Juliet was sitting.

There are three different cameramen on the team, we've realized. And most of the time they carry their cameras on their shoulders when they're filming. But occasionally they actually set up a tripod. That's what they did for the party. And right now there was one tripod with a camera pointing towards the counter, filming what people were choosing to eat, I supposed.

"I was thinking about what you asked, Ems," said Bryony. "Perhaps one of the dinner ladies would know about the domestic bursar. You can find out who it is and where their office is."

"Yes, I'll ask someone when I take my plate back," I said, feeling grateful to Bryony, because I'd told her my plan but I'd been wondering where to start. But just then I heard someone at the next table saying that she had to go to a netball practice and when I glanced at my watch I couldn't believe how quickly the time had gone by. Unless I rushed around at a hundred miles an hour, I wouldn't be able to do a few things at the garden ready for after school, like I'd planned.

"Okay, I'm off!" I said, kicking Sasha by mistake as I got up from the bench. "Sorry, Sash. See you in the garden, everyone." Then I raced over to the counter, nearly dropping my knife and fork in my big hurry.

But when I was almost there, I heard someone mockingly singing a line from the old nursery rhyme: "The farmer wants a wife..."

I made the mistake of glancing over to find out who it was, and saw a grinning Juliet. And that tiny second of not paying attention to where I was going made me knock into the cameraman.

"Whoops! Sorry!" I said. "I didn't see you."

A great guffaw of laughter erupted from Juliet's table.

"That's okay," said the man, grinning at me. "No damage done."

I heard Juliet's voice coming over in a very unsubtle undertone. "Some people will do anything to get attention, won't they?"

And again I was filled with a sharp crossness,

75

which quickly shrivelled and left me hurt and embarrassed and bright red as I handed my plate to one of the dinner ladies.

"Er, excuse me," I asked her quietly, desperately hoping that I couldn't be heard by anyone except her. "Do you know where the domestic bursar's office is, please?"

"Miss Gerard's office?"

Miss Gerard. That was a name I'd heard before. A memory of Ms. Carmichael walking towards me in the corridor beside a very slim, smart lady in high heels flashed through my mind. I remembered those high heels because they seemed so loud compared to everyone else's shoes. And I also remembered how stern and unsmiling the lady looked, even though Ms. Carmichael was saying, "Thank you, Miss Gerard," as they went past.

I nodded at the dinner lady and swallowed. I hadn't realized until this moment that Miss Gerard and the domestic bursar were one and the same person. "Yes, do you know where her office is?"

"Main building. Top floor. Somewhere up there."

"Thank you." I decided to go ahead with my next question even though it was a bit embarrassing having to ask it. "Er...what exactly does domestic bursar mean?"

"She's in charge of the catering, love. Plus she's responsible for how the buildings and grounds get looked after. Sorts out how much gets spent and all that." The dinner lady glanced at the camera as though to check that she wasn't being filmed, then leaned forwards. "Word of advice, love. Choose your moment carefully. That's all I'm saying." Then she nodded firmly and went back to work.

"Th...thank you."

When I went through the gate into the garden, I thought how funny it was that until Saturday, my favourite thing at school had always been to go riding at the local stables, but now my mind was full of gardening. I got the gloves out of the outhouse and set to work straight away. I just planned to move the pile of weeds into the corner, to start a proper compost.

It was so frustrating that there was never enough time at lunchtime and it always got dark so quickly after school, which only left the weekend. And if it rained there was no point in doing anything, because the earth was like a mudbath. At least I could wear wellies at the weekend, though. Not like now. I knew I shouldn't really garden in my uniform, so I was extra careful all the time to make sure I wasn't getting it covered in dirt.

It was very satisfying moving the pile of weeds, because now it could start rotting away and I wouldn't need to disturb it again. I was just wondering whether to quickly pull up a few more, when I suddenly got a lovely surprise at the sound of Stan's voice.

"Hello, Emily!" He was coming through the gap in the hedge from Ms. Carmichael's house, and gave me a little wave as he walked over to me. I noticed he was clutching a small brown bag. "You're certainly a worker, I'll say that for you!" Then his eyes fell to my shoes and he chuckled. "Hope you don't get into trouble!"

I bit my lip. Oh no, my shoes were a real mess. I hadn't meant to get so carried away. I knew I'd have to take them off and hold them under the tap in the loos and wipe them off with paper hand towels like I had done last time.

"I'm not going to be here after school," Stan went on, "so I brought these photos to show you, on the off-chance you'd be here now."

"Oh, great!" I put my spade down and pulled off my gloves.

"Here we are…"

He took them out one at a time and handed them to me. "There, you can see this was a real working garden, can't you?"

The first picture was black and white, but Stan was right – it looked so different from the bare piece of land we were standing on now. There were rows and rows of tall vegetables.

"This next one was taken in winter. About this time of year actually. See, everything's thriving all the same."

It was true. I could just about make out broccoli and sprouts, leeks and onions and one I wasn't sure about. "What's that, Stan?"

"That's swede. I used to love a bit of mashed swede. It went a long way in the kitchen, too." He handed me the last picture. It was in colour, and I gasped at the green that looked so brilliantly bright after the black and white. "This was taken just before that headmistress – Mrs. Cape, that was her name – decided to knock it on the head altogether and bring in all the veggies rather than growing any of our own. Sad day for me. I loved working this garden, I can tell you."

I nodded as I carried on staring at the photo, and thought I could imagine exactly how poor Stan must be feeling now.

"Ah well, there you are," he went on. "That's life. I'm way past retirement age and I've been lucky that Miss Carmichael has kept me on to do her bits and bobs. I'll be sad to finally leave the place for good, come spring."

"You mean, you're leaving at the end of this term?"

"Well before that, actually. Half-term. Just a few more weeks to go. No need for a gardener any more. Miss C has gone crazy-paving mad, so there's only a few tubs and a bit of lawn round her place, and she seems to keep on top of that herself."

"Oh dear." I wished I was a grown-up at that moment, because I felt such a wave of sorrow for Stan and I wanted to say the right thing to help make him feel better. "I'm going to see Miss Gerard, you know, and I'm going to ask her about having more than just this little herb garden. And when it looks like it used to look, I'll ask if I can invite you to come and see!"

"So, that's your plan, is it?" chuckled Stan. "Well I'm glad you're full of spirit, because you'll need it. Nothing against the school in general, but I doubt you'll get past Miss Gerard. She's a tough one." He shook his head sadly.

I thought about Emily Peters and how proud she

would be if I brought her vegetable garden back, and I knew at that moment that I would definitely be brave and face Miss Gerard. I'd be doing it for Emily and for Stan, but also for myself.

Stan and I said goodbye to each other and I asked if he'd be there the next day but he said he only did a few hours' work each week at Silver Spires and he probably wouldn't be back till the following Monday.

"I'll come and find you after school," he told me. Then he looked at his watch. "Aren't you going to be late for lessons?"

I checked the time on my own watch and nearly had a heart attack. I'd been so absorbed with the photos and talking to Stan that I'd done it again. I'd managed to miss the start of afternoon school. This time it was history, but at least it was only Mrs. Egerton, and she's not half so strict as Mr. Pattle.

"I'll clear up here, you get going," said Stan.

So I rushed off at top speed, calling over my shoulder that I'd see him next Monday, and thanking him for showing me the photos and tidying up my tools.

The last sound I heard as I ran along the other side of the tall hedge was Stan's lovely chuckle.

Chapter Six

Waking up the following morning I felt instantly excited but very nervous. I took a quick look round at my friends' beds and saw that, as usual, I was the first one to be awake. I knew I would be, but I really wished that at least Bryony might wake up so I could talk everything through with her.

I was being silly, of course, because I'd already talked and talked to all my friends the day before, and told them about meeting Stan and seeing the photos and how I was determined to try to get Miss Gerard to let me have more land. And that wasn't all. I was going to talk to her about recycling the vegetable and fruit peelings too, so we could use the compost for growing more veggies. I really wanted her to realize that the gardening club was important, and that it was going to be more than just a club. It was going to make Silver Spires a greener place altogether.

Bryony had worn her heaviest frown when I'd told her that last bit, and I always worry when Bryony frowns, because she's so often right about things. I'd told her who Miss Gerard was and what the dinner lady had said about her, and I guess Bryony didn't think I had much chance of getting anywhere with such a scary lady.

"What time is it?" came her sleepy voice out of the gloom. (It wasn't even light outside yet.)

"You've got at least another ten minutes," I whispered. "Go back to sleep, Bry."

"'S okay." She sat up and did a big yawn, then flopped back down again, blinking a bit before she looked directly at me. "Are you sure you don't want me to come with you?"

"No, I'll be fine, honestly."

I wasn't half so confident as I was trying to sound, but I knew this was something I had to do on my own and I'd gone over and over what I was going to say. The six of us had decided that the best time for me to approach Miss Gerard was right at the beginning of the day, before she got too deep into her work. And we'd also found out from Miss Stevenson that Miss Gerard gets into school really early every morning, at about quarter to eight. The plan was that I'd wait in the main building in the big reception hall, and when I heard Miss Gerard's footsteps come clicking across the hall and up the stairs, I'd give it two minutes, then go upstairs after her and knock on her door.

It all seemed so simple when we'd been working it out, but now that it was almost time to put the plan into action, I was really nervous. And there was something making me even tenser. While we'd all been sitting on my bed talking about it the night before, I'd suddenly thought about the way Miss Gerard's shoes clicked, and I'd found myself calling her Miss Click instead of Miss Gerard, which had given us all a massive fit of the giggles. After that, the others had started saying Miss Click too, until it had kind of stuck. So now I was worried I might call her that by mistake while I was actually having my meeting with her, which would be totally disastrous.

In the shower I went over what I was going to say to Miss Gerard one more time. It felt like I was learning lines for a play or something, but I knew it was best to have something actually prepared, as I was so nervous. As usual, though, my mind wandered off after no time at all, and I found myself thinking back to Emily Peters and Stan. I wondered whether Stan had sent one of his photos to Emily yet and whether she was imagining me working away in my garden, trying to get it back to how it was. Whenever I got to thinking about that, I always wanted to hurry everything up so I could write and tell Emily it was all happening and it was great. But I knew that wasn't possible. You can't hurry nature. It has its own plan that no one should interfere with. That's what my dad says anyway.

I can remember one time when we were driving the tractor home together late one night in the half-term holiday last May.

"You get the ground ready and you sow the seeds, Ems," he said. "And from little seeds come big results, you know. The secret is keeping in tune with nature's plan. That's the secret."

I love it when Dad says things like that to me. Somehow, they always stick in my mind. If our teachers said such interesting things, I'd be in top sets for everything. Not that we're actually in sets for all the subjects – just science, maths and English – but still, it would be nice to be in top sets for just one of those three things. My science teacher did say she was very pleased with my work on soil recently, though, so maybe I'll get put up a set for that subject next term. I really enjoyed the work on soil, because I love anything to do with the environment. But geography is probably my best subject, even though I don't like what we're doing at the moment on maps. I prefer work on different types of land, like deserts and jungle and marshes and things. I quite like history too, especially as Mrs. Egerton is so laid-back. I think she's a bit of a scatterbrain, actually. Or maybe she's a dreamer, like me. She must be one or the other, anyway, because Bryony said she didn't even notice I wasn't in the lesson yesterday. So at least that's one thing I don't have to worry about.

By the time I was showered and dressed, all the others were awake, and I felt really honoured, because every single one of them offered to come with me to see Miss Gerard.

"Sorry, guys!" I told them a bit shakily. "This is something just for me."

"See you at breakfast then, Ems," they called, as I went off with my heart thudding like a bass drum. "Good luck!"

* * *

The words of my speech were still whizzing around in my mind as I walked along, breathing in the cold morning air and trying to keep calm. I looked up at the pale streaky sky and noticed that there was a bit of dim yellow sun pushing through. Straight away my eyes went to the spires, but they weren't silver yet. Maybe they would be later. And that made me think of Emily again. I never did get round to asking her whether she and her friends used to watch the sun make the spires gleam, like we do.

The other reason I love the main building is because it's so huge and grand and old. The only thing I don't like about it is that it's a bit dark for me. The furniture is dark, the beams are dark, and the little diamond windowpanes don't let in as much light as big windowpanes do – although there are lots of them, so that helps lighten it a bit.

At twenty to eight in the morning the building also seems deserted, and I felt as though I was trespassing as I stood staring at the noticeboard in the main reception hall. If anyone had been watching me they'd think I was trying to memorize every single word or something, but I didn't know what else to do as I waited for Miss Gerard to arrive.

The clock in the hall said exactly seven forty-five when I heard the front door open. I didn't turn round, just stood there, stiff with tension. I knew straight away that it was Miss Gerard from the click of her shoes on the flagstones, and immediately a nervous giggle rose in my throat. Actually it was awful that she was so punctual. It just seemed to make her all the scarier, somehow.

The clicks went all the way up the dark oak stairs and seemed to echo round the whole building. I could even hear her clicking along the top corridor, and then there was the click of her door shutting.

I swallowed and started counting in what I thought were seconds. When I'd got to a hundred and twenty I made my way upstairs and crept along the corridor, looking at all the doors. The one on the end had a plaque on it that said *DOMESTIC BURSAR*. As I stood outside I felt as though my heartbeat was the loudest thing happening in the whole building. I knocked gently, but there was no reply. She couldn't have heard me, so I knocked a bit more loudly and this time she said, "Yes, come in!" in a bit of a snappy voice.

I opened the door, anxious already that I'd got off to a bad start, and swallowed as my eyes took in the size of the office. Miss Gerard was sitting in a smart office chair on wheels at a huge desk, working on her computer, and I noticed how straight her back was.

I also noticed her silky shirt, her smart jacket, her hair in a perfect bob, and the crisp expression on her face – there was no other word for it. In that second I wished I could turn and run away, because it seemed more obvious than ever that someone with an important job like domestic bursar would take no notice at all of a student who'd only been at Silver Spires for a term and a bit.

"Can I help you?" she said, and her eyes said, *I'm very busy and I'm waiting for you, so could you make it snappy?*

It was too late to run away now. "I'm sorry to disturb you, but..." I said, and then something flashed into my mind. Maybe I should ask for an appointment to talk to her, so then she'd be expecting me and there'd be time for me to explain about everything. Yes, that's what I'd do.

Just say it, Emily...

"I was wondering if I could make an appointment to see you..."

She did something with her lips that made her look as though she was pouting but I realized this must be her expression for thinking hard, because she stayed silent for a few seconds as she slowly moved her glasses till they were balancing on the tip of her nose. Then she spoke in a rush, with all the crispness from her face coming out in her voice. "I think it might be better if you just tell me what it's about."

"Er..." It was now or never. "Well, you see, I wanted to talk to you about..." My brain was whirring away, trying to remember what I'd decided to say first. "Er, you see, I'm interested in growing vegetables, because we do that at home and I'm used to it. And I was wondering about growing vegetables at Silver Spires. I mean...vegetables that we could actually eat..." Oh dear, this was coming out completely wrong. I'd better get to the point. "I know Tony asked if I could have a bit of land, but..."

She took off her glasses altogether then, and leaned back in her chair. "Yes, that's right, and I told Tony to go ahead and allocate you a small plot."

"Only...I was wondering if I could have a bit more, please, because—"

She tapped her glasses on her lip. "As I understand it, you want to start a gardening club. Is that right?"

"Yes...a big one..."

She was sounding very brisk. "Well I might be able to extend it a little. I'd have to have a word with Tony." She reached for a notepad and pen. "And perhaps I ought to speak to your housemistress. Which house are you in?"

"Forest Ash, but—"

"Name?

"Emily Dowd, but—"

"Year?"

"Seven."

"Mrs. Pridham's the housemistress, isn't she?"

"Yes, only—

She was scribbling on her notepad. "I'll ask her to let you know when I've had a word with Tony. I'm not making any promises, and it'll take a few days because I've got a lot on at the moment and it'll have to work its way up the list." She put her glasses back on and looked over the top of them at me. "All right?"

My brain was spinning. *No, no, it's not all right. I want more than just a little extra land. I want a proper compost, using food waste from the kitchens. And I want to change the whole way of catering at Silver Spires.*

But how could I say that? Miss Gerard would stop listening before I got halfway through the first sentence. Maybe I ought to just keep quiet and go away. I tried to think what Bryony would do. I could practically hear her voice in my ear…

Just accept the extra bit of land, Ems, then come back in a few days when you've started the club properly.

I knew it made sense but I didn't think I'd have

the courage to come back another time. It was now or never.

Speak, Emily. Just SPEAK!

"Er...I really wanted to ask about growing vegetables for us all...to actually eat...at Silver Spires."

Her forehead seemed to suddenly jut forwards and her mouth pursed right up. At least she wasn't scribbling any more or firing questions at me.

I forced my brain to concentrate on the words I'd planned. "Er...you see, I know the school used to grow all its own vegetables, and now that everyone's trying to go green, I thought Silver Spires could too." It had sounded mature when I'd tried it in front of the mirror, but here under the gaze of Miss Click, it sounded really babyish. The expression on her face told me that I hadn't got much longer to speak, so I gabbled the rest and kept falling over my words. "Fruit and vegetable peelings and apple cores could be turned into compost for the garden and you might have to still order a few things from outside but there are always enough seasonal vegetables so we could grow most of them here and—"

"Whoa! Hold it!" She gave me a kind of half smile. "There's the small question of manpower for a plan like this. In a nutshell, Emily, because I don't have much time: it's very laudable that you've thought about all this, but it would be far too labour-intensive. It would cost just as much, if not more, to grow food for as many girls as we have here. And we can't rely on students for something of such economic consequence. I don't expect you to understand the big picture, but there it is. Now—"

"It used to work fifty years ago. The students were keen then. I think we could make it happen again. In fact, I'm sure we could."

I'd given myself a bit of a shock by interrupting like that and I swallowed and waited nervously.

The crisp look was right back. "I'm sorry, Emily. I can see exactly where you're coming from. But the answer is no." She drew a deep breath, as though she knew she'd got a lot to say and she was determined to fit it all into one breath. "The school decided to go down the route of buying in its fruit and vegetables many years ago and it's proved easier, quicker and more reliable. And on the question of recycling the peelings, rotting them down into compost is a long process and it's also horribly smelly. So, for all those reasons, I'm afraid your idea is simply not an option now at Silver Spires."

She gave me a semi-smile, then took another breath. "However, perhaps you're still interested in expanding your patch just a little for the gardening club?" She was doing the pouting thing again, only this time her eyebrows were arched right up in a big question mark. And she was on her feet too. My time really was up. And my head was spinning as she fixed me with her questioning gaze.

If I say yes she'll think I'm happy with nothing more than a little gardening club, and yet I'm so not.

But how am I ever going to get what I want unless I start somewhere?

"Yes…please."

"Excellent. Leave it with me." She walked to the door and held it open for me.

"Thank you."

"That's all right."

Click. The door shut. My time was up.

I felt such an idiot telling the others over breakfast about my great meeting with Miss Gerard.

"Everything I said came out wrong and it was totally in the wrong order and she finished up by thinking I was happy with just a bit more land for my gardening club."

"So didn't you get the chance to tell her about wanting to grow vegetables for use in the school?" asked Izzy gently.

"I tried but she wouldn't stop interrupting." I sighed a big sigh. "And I obviously didn't say the right things to make her realize how important it was," I said miserably. "She just went on about how much quicker and easier it was to buy in the vegetables and it was obvious that nothing I was ever going to say would make her change her mind."

"Poor Ems," said Antonia.

I sighed again as I thought back to my disastrous meeting. Then I spoke quickly, because I'd had enough of talking about it now.

"And she said that composts were smelly and took ages. And I said it had been done here before and she said I didn't get the big picture. The end." I folded my arms and dropped my shoulders forwards in despair, which made all my friends murmur that I mustn't worry and it would all turn out right in the end, and things like that.

"Poor Ems," repeated Antonia.

"At least she's letting you have a bit more land. And in time you might be able to expand even more when you show everyone what you can do," said Nicole.

"Just take it one step at a time," Bryony added.

When Bryony said that I felt much better. Of course I should just keep working away in the garden to make it look amazing. And better still, I must definitely go ahead with trying to get other people interested in joining the gardening club.

"I should have asked Stan if I could hang on to his photo, shouldn't I? Then I could have made photocopies and put them up all over the place with information about the gardening club. I'll ask him next time I see him, because I need to spread the word, don't I?"

I looked round at my friends, feeling myself cheering up like mad, but the looks on their faces sent me right back into the doldrums. "What?" I asked Bryony. "Why are you all looking at me like that?"

"Jet's already been spreading the word," explained Izzy, giving me a sad smile. "She casually asked where you were just now before you got here, and Bryony told her to mind her own business, but she's got a thing about you for some reason, and since she heard about your gardening idea...well..."

I felt myself getting cross as I looked round the dining hall for Juliet.

"She's gone now," said Antonia quietly.

"What did she say about me?" I had to know.

"Oh...she was just horrible and...sarcastic," said Sasha. "But don't worry, we all stuck up for you."

I could tell that my friends were trying to be kind by not telling me and in the end I turned to Bryony. "Tell me what she said. Please, Bry."

Bryony took a deep breath. "Okay, I'll tell you, but you mustn't get upset. She's not worth it."

I nodded and waited.

"She said something like, 'Emily's probably single-handedly digging up the whole grounds and making the school into one massive vegetable garden so we can all be the greenest people on earth. Maybe we should all take mudbaths.'" And as Bryony spoke, I could just hear Juliet saying something mean and nasty like that.

I sighed a deep sigh. "Do you think she'll put people off joining the club?"

"Maybe some people...at first," said Bryony. "But *we'll* all help you, so you don't have to worry."

"Yes, you can count on us," said Antonia, which I thought was sweet.

After that our conversation turned to the TV people, because apparently they'd been filming in the hall at Forest Ash when the others had left for breakfast, and some Year Nine girls further along our table were talking about how they'd even been filmed in lessons.

"Imagine if they'd come into the history lesson that I missed," I whispered to Bryony, feeling myself tensing up at the thought.

"Was it hard to act naturally?" Izzy asked the Year Nines.

"It was at first," a girl called Lottie said. "But after a bit, you just forget the camera's there," she added. "So it was okay, I suppose."

I started to wonder whether I'd acted naturally on the times when I'd been filmed myself. I knew I definitely had done when I'd been with Emily and Stan, because I was so interested to hear all that they were saying. I wasn't so sure that I'd seemed natural on Sunday morning before breakfast, though, when Bryony and I had been looking for Tony. And as for when the cameraman filmed me in the garden... At least I'd been wearing my tracky bums at the time, and not my school uniform, thank goodness. I would have looked really stupid in the middle of a great big patch of old wasteland, digging away, getting myself all messed up.

Mum and Dad would probably be pleased with me, though, if they saw me in the film. I could just picture our family crammed into Aunty Mandy's little living room, all eyes on her TV screen, watching me crouching over a pile of weeds. Aunty Mandy would definitely think I was completely bonkers. She's the complete opposite of Mum and Dad. She lives in a first-floor flat in a bustling little town and she doesn't have any garden at all, just a big balcony...

Wait a minute... Something was straining to get out of my mind into the open. What was it Mum said to Aunty Mandy on the phone in the Christmas holidays? *"You ought to get yourself a wormery, Mand. Then at least you'd be doing something green. You can recycle all your food waste into compost, and then you can grow lovely herbs in pots on your balcony."* I can remember Mum explaining to Aunty Mandy that a wormery is a plastic or wooden container that's full of composting worms, which eat and live on the decaying foods on the surface, and turn it into compost, just like that.

Yes! That was it. That's what Silver Spires needed. A wormery. And Miss Gerard might approve of that idea. It didn't take ages for the compost to develop in one of those, after all, and I was sure it wouldn't smell because Aunty Mandy would never put up with something smelly. A wormery might be quite popular too, as it would be interesting to watch the composting actually happening before our eyes. And people would realize that gardening is more fun than they thought, and then Juliet wouldn't get away with saying horrible sarcastic things any more. Plus, even better, we'd have loads of compost to grow more vegetables with.

Yes, a wormery was what Silver Spires needed. And *I* would be the one to get them one. I'd wait till the end of school, then I'd go and research them thoroughly on the internet.

Yes!!!

Chapter Seven

All through lessons that day I could think of nothing but my latest composting idea. I had four tellings-off for not concentrating and I deserved every one of them because my mind was a million miles away from square roots and litmus tests and tectonic plates and the Tower of London, as my brain space was totally being used up on wormeries.

I thought it would probably be best to try and get Mrs. Pridham interested and then she could ask Miss Click about it, because there was no way I'd dare to go back to see Miss Click so soon after my last meeting with her. I'd been tempted to rush back to Forest Ash at lunchtime to look up wormeries on the internet and talk to Mrs. Pridham about getting one, but I knew there wouldn't be time, as I also wanted to go over to my garden just in case Stan happened to be around, so I could ask him if I could borrow one of his photos. I knew from what he'd said about only doing very few hours' work at school each week that he wasn't likely to be there, but I was still disappointed when he didn't show up.

It was a relief when the bell for the end of afternoon school finally went, and I was free to shoot out of the classroom and over to Forest Ash at top speed.

On the internet I found loads of sites about wormeries and I studied them all carefully so Mrs. Pridham would be impressed with my thorough research. It was a question of finding the most suitable type of wormery for Silver Spires. We needed something really big to go outside at the back of the kitchens so the dinner ladies could compost all the food scraps, and then we also needed two or three small wheelie bins in central places around the Silver Spires grounds for us girls to chuck our apple cores and things into. It would be easy to wheel the bins round to the wormery. And then I read that you could recycle old newspapers in wormeries too. Yes, of course, because paper comes from trees. I'd never thought of that.

"Hi, Ems, I've been looking for you all over the place!" Bryony had come into the internet room and was trying to see what was fascinating me so much on the screen. "I never thought I'd find you in here!"

I jumped up and grabbed her hands. "Good news!"

She gave me one of her frowns. "Why do I get the feeling I'm about to hear about a brand new crazy Em-plan...?" She pulled her hands away, peered at the screen and started reading. "*These worms differ from normal garden worms in that they eat and live on the decaying food on the surface*... Mmm...sounds charming. So their pooh is the compost?"

I couldn't help laughing at the look of disgust on Bryony's face. "Yes – it's no different from using horse manure as a compost."

"So what does the actual wormery look like?"

"Like a dustbin or a big bucket and you can get ones that look like trays stacked up. There are all different kinds and it's exactly what we need here at Silver Spires!" I told her in a gabble. "I'm going to order one off the internet. Everyone will love it, because you can see it working right before your eyes, and the worms leave behind a fantastic compost, really high in nutrients. That means that when it gets dug back into the ground to grow more vegetables, they'll be so much better for us all to eat than the stuff we usually have…"

Bryony suddenly put her hands up like a policeman stopping traffic. "Ems, Ems, hang on a sec! How are you going to afford it?"

It was actually quite a nice surprise when Bryony said that, because what I'd thought she was going to point out was that Miss Gerard had already told me she wasn't changing the way Silver Spires worked, and hearing that out loud would have really spoiled my dream for good.

"Er…" How *was* I going to afford it? I hadn't thought about that. I racked my brains hard. "Er…"

I felt myself starting to deflate, but I so wanted to stay on my high, so I blurted out my thoughts as they jumped into my head. "I could save and save… No, that'd take too long… Mum and Dad might agree to raising my allowance…" Bryony was shaking her head. She must have known I was clutching at straws. "What about if I sold something?" It felt as though I'd caught a glimpse of a little chink of light at the end of the tunnel. "Yes, I could sell that pink top that Aunty Mand got me when I was into pink. It's too tight now anyway."

Bryony was frowning again.

I had to think harder. "And I'm sure I could find other stuff to sell... Wh...what about you, Bry? Have you got any clothes you don't really want?"

Bryony's frown lifted when I said that, which was so lovely, because I hadn't really thought it was much of an idea at all, but she started nodding slowly and thoughtfully. "Yes, that's a good idea. We could have a clothes sale. I bet people wouldn't mind donating clothes they didn't like any more or whatever. And everyone would definitely love buying new clothes for themselves, and all the money could go towards your wormery."

"Bry, you're a genius!"

"No, *you* thought of it!"

I could have pretended that was true, but I'd never lie to Bryony, not even a white lie. "No, I was actually only thinking of you and me selling our clothes. I never thought about anyone else!"

"Well, I've got nothing and your top's very nice, Ems, but I doubt it would raise enough for a wormery! How much does one cost anyway?"

"Depends. Small ones are about twenty-five

pounds, I think it said on one website, but we'd need a really big one – plus the wheelie bins."

We were looking up prices on the internet when Antonia and Nicole came in and asked us what was so interesting.

"We're researching Emily's latest plan," Bryony replied, looking mysterious. "Listen to this!"

She did a grand gesture with her hands and grinned at me as though I was about to make a big announcement.

"Well," I began excitedly, "I've been finding out about wormeries, and they're brilliant for recycling food waste and I reckon the school could do with at least one. And we're going to hold a clothes sale to raise the money!"

"Hey, great!" said Nicole straight away.

"Yes, great..." echoed Antonia with a puzzled look on her face. "Er...I've got quite a few clothes I can sell for your wormery thing."

It was so sweet of her to want to help me when it was obvious she didn't really understand where the money was going, and probably hadn't ever come across the word "worm" before. So I explained a bit more and she wrinkled up her nose in disgust.

"What does Mrs. Pridham think about it?" asked Nicole.

There was another silence while I took in what she'd just said and realized that, actually, I had a long way to go before I could get my wormery.

Nicole was really frowning now. "You *have* asked her about the clothes sale, haven't you?"

I shook my head. "I've only just thought of the plan." I glanced at my watch. It was nearly time for supper.

"Better leave it till later," said Bryony, reading my mind. "I'll come with you if you want."

"Thanks, Bry."

There were a few minutes between supper and prep and I couldn't make myself wait till prep was over, so I persuaded Bryony that we should go to see Mrs. Pridham straight after we'd eaten. I was a bit nervous when she opened the door looking flustered, because I needed her in a good mood, not a flustered one, when I talked to her about wormeries and the clothes sale. On the other hand, perhaps if she was a bit distracted and busy she might just quickly say, "Yes, that's fine" to get rid of us.

Her glasses were on the top of her head, kind of stuffed crookedly in her hair, making it stick up on one side.

"Yes, girls, what can I do for you? Is it something that can wait? It's not the best time right now…"

She was trying to smile but it wasn't working very well.

"We can come back—" Bryony started to say, but I interrupted her, speaking in one of my top-speed gabbles.

"It was just to ask you if it would be all right to hold a clothes sale in aid of a wormery for recycling for the school. It would be really good – really environmentally friendly and green. You put your apple cores and banana peel in it and the worms turn it into compost, and then we can use the compost for growing vegetables."

Mrs. Pridham's eyes were very wide, as though she hadn't a clue what I was talking about, and I noticed Bryony suddenly seemed to be standing very close to me. She was tapping my leg and I guessed it was to tell me to be quiet. Instantly I regretted my big mouth. I'd probably put Mrs. Pridham off the idea by talking about it when she was obviously trying to deal with something else.

"So this is…for your gardening club?" she asked, still looking confused.

"Yes, yes…for the gardening club," I said, giving her a bright smile.

"Right, and Tony thinks it's a good idea? Or is it something you've thought of yourself?"

"I haven't mentioned it to Tony yet...but I'm sure he'd agree...because it's like recycling paper, only it's for food waste."

"They're very common. You can buy them very easily off the internet," said Bryony. Already Mrs. Pridham was looking a bit less confused. "So we just need to check that it's okay for us to organize a clothes sale to pay for it," Bryony went on. "Just a small sale one weekend where girls could bring along a top or a belt or something they didn't want any more and people would buy the stuff to raise the money for the wormery. Emerald dorm will organize the whole thing."

Mrs. Pridham's face had completely lost its bewildered look. "Yes, that sounds all right, on the face of it," she said, glancing at her watch. She seemed to understand Bryony so much better than me. Why was I so terrible at explaining things? Then it was just as though she'd gone back to whatever she was thinking about before we knocked at her door, because her eyes were all distracted again. "Let's talk about it properly when I have a little more time." She was starting to close the door. "Sorry, girls..."

"That's okay, we'll be getting the posters organized," said Bryony. "Can we have it here at Forest Ash? In the common room?"

"Maybe, of the two common rooms, the break-out room would be better," said Mrs. Pridham, "as there are some spare trestle tables in there you could use. I'll have a think."

"Okay, thanks, Mrs. Pridham."

"Yes, thanks, Mrs. Pridham," I echoed.

And then she shut the door and left us standing there.

We stayed quite still and silent for a few seconds, then slowly turned to each other, smiling. Well, Bryony was smiling. I was grinning my head off.

Chapter Eight

"Look, this is a general noticeboard," said Izzy. "It'll be fine to put it up here."

The six of us were in the reception area of the swimming pool building. We'd already put up two posters about the clothes sale – one in the corridor outside the dining hall and one in the hall of the main building – and it was only eight o'clock on Friday morning.

I'd felt really happy when all my friends got into the idea of the clothes sale so quickly. Bryony and I had explained about our chat with Mrs. Pridham, and then straight after prep the six of us had grabbed some sheets of A3 from the printer in the internet room. The next day we'd got into pairs and whenever we could grab a moment we worked on posters announcing the sale that was taking place in the break-out room at Forest Ash at three o'clock on Sunday. Nicole had wondered whether it might have been better to leave it till the following weekend to give everyone enough time to see the posters, but I'd said no because I was in my usual hurry now my new plan had started to take shape, and I just had the feeling that I must get on with it as soon as possible. After all, the sooner we had the sale, the sooner we'd be able to order the wormery, and then the sooner I could get the food recycling started. And once the teachers saw the recycling working so well, there was bound to be more chance that they'd get into the whole growing-vegetables-on-the-premises thing. I'd also taken the chance to mention the "great new gardening club" that was starting up, and asked for anyone interested to see Emily Dowd.

At the bottom of the posters there was information about bringing your unwanted clothes to the break-out room at Forest Ash by one o'clock this Sunday, and that the money was going to a very worthy cause. Nicole and Izzy both thought it would be better to actually mention what the money from the sale was going towards, in case people thought I was keeping it for myself or something, but the rest of us were anxious that if we mentioned a wormery some girls might not completely get what that was, or think it was silly, or might even think it was a joke. It was such a good idea of Bryony's to just put that the money was going to a worthy cause instead.

But as we put up Sasha and Izzy's poster, I had the same twinges of guilt that I'd felt when we'd been sticking the other two up, because Mrs. Pridham hadn't exactly given us permission for this clothes sale. She'd said she was going to have a think about it. She *had* said the idea was fine on the face of it, though, and she'd even suggested that the break-out room would be better than the common room, so that was practically saying we could go ahead, wasn't it? And she was perfectly happy with the wormery idea when we told her it was for my gardening club. So, as we admired the lovely bright poster on the wall in the swimming pool building, I told myself to stop being silly. Then my stomach did an enormous rumble, reminding us that it was time for breakfast, and we made for the door.

"What's this?" came a voice from just behind us, as we were about to go outside.

I turned to see Juliet and her friends coming out of the changing room. But it was a girl called Mel who'd spotted our poster. Juliet was looking at her mobile, and I knew I ought to go before she saw me, but I couldn't stop myself from hanging back to hear what she said about the clothes sale.

"Oh great, it's my mum," she announced, still reading the text.

"Oh, is it something about your birthday?" asked one of her friends.

"Certainly is!" she replied, looking mysterious. Then she broke into a wide smile. "Mum's having a massive five-tiered cake delivered, guys. So Oakley's the place to be on Saturday afternoon! I expect it'll be the best party that our boarding house has ever known." A second later her expression turned into a mixture of half bored and half sulky as her eye caught the poster. "So what's this, then?"

A girl called Adelaide noticed us lot hanging about by the door and asked, "Which one of you lot put this up? Was it Emily Dowd, by any chance?"

"Yes it was!" I said. And the moment the words were out of my mouth I regretted them.

"We *all* put it up," Bryony quickly said. Then she jerked her head and gave me a look as if to say, *Come on, let's go*.

But Jet's mocking voice stopped me from moving even a centimetre. *In aid of a worthy cause,* she read out loud. "Hmmm, I wonder what that might be? The Emily Dowd Is *Very* Green fund?"

I thought she was going to say something much more insulting than that, so it was quite a relief that she'd only more or less come out with the truth. I turned to follow Bryony.

But then Adelaide burst out laughing. "Green! Oh, *I* get it!"

"What?" I asked, turning round impulsively.

The rest of her friends were all killing themselves, and I knew I should have just ignored them and walked away, but I hated to think that they were making fun of me, and it made it ten times worse that I didn't even get the joke. I looked at Nicole to see whether she'd got it, as she's really quick to catch on to things, and I could tell she did and she was cross, because she was giving Juliet a real evil. So was Bryony.

"What's so wrong with being green?" I asked, trying to sound as confident as possible.

Well, that made the Year Eights fall about laughing even more.

"Depends which sort of green you're talking about," said Juliet, running her fingers through her hair as she pushed past me. Then: "Somehow I don't think you'll get many girls coming," she said, pushing the door open. "Why should anyone want to hand over their money when they don't even know what you're spending it on? I know I wouldn't!"

"What did she mean? I didn't get her!" I asked, the moment she'd gone off with her friends, rushing because there were cameras not far away.

"The word 'green' means 'naïve', as well as meaning 'environmentally friendly'," Nicole explained quietly as we slowly left the building, following at a distance behind Juliet and her friends. I noticed Juliet's hair was swinging from side to side like a pendulum on a clock and I wondered if she'd had to perfect a certain way of walking to make it do that.

"What is *wrong* with that girl?" Bryony asked through clenched teeth. But then she answered her own question. "It's all because of that time when the cameras followed you and Emily out of the party, and she didn't know where you were going and you wouldn't tell her and so the spotlight wasn't on *her* for once."

"Well I'm not going to let her get to me," I said firmly, even though I was feeling uncomfortable inside. It's not very nice when someone's horrible to you the whole time.

Antonia looked cross. "I don't like the way her friends all...what do you say in English...you know, they are too much of a friend to Jet?"

"They suck up to her," said Bryony flatly. "That's what we say."

We were a despondent little group walking over to breakfast, but we'd cheered up by the time we got our food, because in the queue we heard quite a few people talking about the clothes sale and saying how great it was going to be. Then, when we were sitting down, there seemed to be even more people talking about it. Everyone was saying that they'd got something or other to bring along to sell and there was lots of chatter about how cool it would be to get new clothes for not much money and without even having to go shopping.

Only two days to go! At last something good was happening.

I woke up on Saturday morning with the lovely feeling I always have when it's the weekend and I've only got morning lessons to get through before I can do what I want. I leaped out of bed and went over to the window. Good, it looked as though it had only rained a bit during the night, so the ground wouldn't be too soaked. And already there was a pale sun winking at me through the clouds. I felt a bit sad that I'd decided to miss riding just this once, but the garden was so important to me, and I badly wanted to use the time to get it properly started. Also, I wouldn't have to put up with Jet showing off, or making fun of me, or both.

As soon as lessons finished, we six had a quick lunch, then went over to the garden and set to work. My friends were brilliant. They didn't really have much idea of what they were supposed to do, but once I'd showed them, they seemed to really enjoy it. The only trouble was that it started to drizzle, and after a while we were all beginning to get soaked. I could tell that Antonia and Izzy were fed up, so in the end I told them not to worry about carrying on any longer.

"We've done really well," I said. "I just want to get this massive root out, and then we can call it a day."

"But it's a root. Why will you call it 'a day'?" asked Antonia, her eyebrows knitted in confusion.

We all burst out laughing and as Nicole explained what the expression "call it a day" meant, I bent down and tugged like mad at the root that was sticking up. I pulled and pulled, but it seemed to be buried deep in the ground, and it was really annoying me. "Can someone help…?"

Bryony immediately picked up the spade and started digging all around the area where the root was stuck, while the others watched with interest and I kept pulling. Bit by bit she was releasing more and more of the root, and when it finally came out altogether, and I nearly fell over backwards, Nicole punched the air and said, "Yesss!" and the others all cheered.

"Teamwork!" I said, high-fiving Bryony.

We trooped back to Forest Ash feeling really dirty but happy, and on the way we had a lovely surprise, because the sun came out properly and for a moment there was a beautiful rainbow in the sky.

Antonia and Nicole rushed ahead to look at the spires on the main building and when we caught up, sure enough, they were sparkling bright, and I felt so happy to belong to such a lovely place as this school.

But a moment later my happiness came crashing down.

"Emily! My flat. Now!"

I turned to see a furious Mrs. Pridham right behind us. My heart seemed to stretch as she fixed me with an icy glare and then walked off, her footsteps stamping out an angry trail that led to Forest Ash.

"Oh, Ems!" whispered Sasha as the others stared at me with big eyes, except for Bryony, who frowned hard at the ground.

I bit my lip and followed Mrs. Pridham.

Chapter Nine

"**I** cannot believe that one of *my* girls from *my* boarding house is *so* naïve that she imagines she can skip lessons willy-nilly and no one will notice. Just because the teachers don't treat you like infants and take a register after lunch, Emily, doesn't mean that they aren't fully aware of who is present and who is absent."

Mrs. Pridham and I were sitting in upright chairs in a room in Mrs. Pridham's flat that I'd never been in before, like a tiny office, and I felt stupid and ashamed. My friends had warned me I could get in trouble and they were so right.

"Mrs. Egerton came to see me just now. She'd noted your absence in her history lesson on Tuesday and told me that she knew there'd be a good reason. However she'd not been able to follow it up because she'd been on a course since then, so her first opportunity to mention it to me was this morning, and she just wanted to check you were all right." Mrs. Pridham's eyes flashed in a sort of scornful way and she spoke a bit more loudly, stressing some of the words more than normal. "Mr. *Pattle* heard us *talking* and mentioned that you'd missed *geography* on Monday, but that you'd *explained* your *absence* in his next lesson by saying you'd been *stuck* in the *loo* feeling *sick*." The angry look Mrs. Pridham was giving me was really making me feel sick now. I felt myself shrivelling inside as she carried on. It was all the more shocking because the actual words she was saying weren't horrible at all, it was just the way she was saying them. "At this point, *another* teacher chimed in, saying that she'd seen you *racing along* towards the *language lab* on Monday, and I've looked at the timetable, and this was when you were *supposed to be suffering with a stomach ache*! What is going on, Emily? What were you doing when you should have been in class?"

I hung my head and felt a lump in my throat.

This was going to be the worst bit.

"I was...gardening..."

There was a moment's silence, then Mrs. Pridham's voice seemed to have grown weaker somehow. "Gardening?"

I nodded.

"You missed lessons because you were *gardening*?"

"Yes," I managed miserably.

The crossness was right back in Mrs. Pridham's voice and when I looked up I saw it in her eyes too. "I can't believe what I'm hearing! Just because you've started a gardening club, it doesn't mean you're free to break rules and garden whenever you want, Emily."

I sat very still, dreading what was to come.

"Well, you'll have to go and see Mr. Pattle and Mrs. Egerton to apologize, and I expect they'll both give you a detention..." She paused and pursed her lips, then took a breath, and I knew there was more to come. "But now, Emily, something *else* has come to my attention. It seems that you and Bryony have gone ahead and put up notices about a clothes sale to take place tomorrow, despite the fact that you know very well I hadn't given permission for it. I can't believe you've acted like this. And I think it's clear that it's not Bryony who is the ringleader."

I swallowed. "Sorry."

"Sorry isn't good enough. I am incredibly disappointed in you, Emily. I find your behaviour underhand and...odious."

I'd never heard the word "odious" before, but I knew it must be something really horrible and I could feel tears gathering behind my eyes. I hated myself for having acted so stupidly and for upsetting Mrs. Pridham so badly. Why couldn't I have just waited for her to tell us it was all right to go ahead with the clothes sale? Why did I have to rush everything?

"Have you got anything to say for yourself, Emily?"

"I..."

"Yes?"

"No."

Mrs. Pridham's eyes were really boring into me, but then she suddenly leaned back in her chair and shook her head slowly. "Well, it looks as though you've learned your lesson, but this can't go unpunished, Emily. As I said, you'll go and see Mrs. Egerton and Mr. Pattle, and they'll no doubt give you detentions. I'd like to stop the clothes sale altogether really, but that would be punishing others who've done nothing wrong, and I know there's a lot of excitement about the sale. However, the money will go to a charity now. I'll sort that out myself. But..." She paused and my heart did that stretching thing again. "If you can't be responsible, then I'm afraid your punishment from me is no more gardening club. Is that clear?"

A tear that had formed in my left eye rolled down my cheek. And as I nodded, a few more fell down too.

"All right then, Emily. You can go now."

It was horrible going up to the dorm and seeing Bryony and the others watching my face so carefully as I went through the door. They were all standing or sitting like statues and seemed to be raising their eyebrows, except for Sasha, who gave me a sad smile. Maybe she could see I'd been crying, even though I hadn't shed a single tear since I'd left Mrs. Pridham's flat.

"I've got to give up the gardening club," I said, as I climbed the ladder up to my cabin bed and flopped back onto it.

A gasp went up from my friends and immediately they all clambered up the ladder and told me to move up a bit so there'd be enough room for us all.

"Truth talk," said Antonia. "Truth talk, Emmy. We'll help you find the answer."

Then I did cry. Because there *was* no answer.

It rained and rained for the rest of the afternoon. Before supper, Bryony and I walked around Silver Spires in our wellies, with the hoods up on our coats. There wasn't a soul in sight and we guessed everyone was probably in their boarding houses or maybe at Oakley at Juliet's birthday party. As we walked past the main building, we actually came across Mr. Pattle getting into his car, and Bryony thought I ought to speak to him straight away to get it over with.

I was dreading what he'd say, but, as it happened, he wasn't half as mad as I'd thought he'd be and just said he could tell I was sorry and that was the most important thing. So then we thought it might be a good idea to go and find Mrs. Egerton too, and in the end, after asking a few people, we tracked her down in the main library.

Things are often the complete opposite to what you're expecting them to be, and this afternoon certainly turned out like that, because Mrs. Egerton was furious and gave me a detention to do after school on Monday. She said she was very disappointed in me, and then she shook her head slowly as though she couldn't think of another thing to say to such a terrible person.

That was the final horrible happening in a day of horrible happenings, and it was a doubly bad one, because I'd been so looking forward to seeing Stan on Monday, and now it looked as though I wouldn't be able to.

On Sunday morning it was still pouring down, and by lunchtime I felt as though the whole world was against me. We'd kept checking the break-out room all morning, but not one single person had brought along any clothes or accessories or anything for our great sale, and I began to get neurotic and to wonder whether Juliet had been at work, persuading people not to come. Actually, I didn't really care whether or not we sold any clothes any more, because there was no reason for this sale now that I'd lost my gardening club. Only it *did* still matter in a way. Just to make me feel as though *something* in my life was working.

So it was a nice surprise when, very gradually, people started to turn up, and belts and shoes and scarves and tops and even jewellery began to pour into the break-out room at Forest Ash. For a while, all six of us had to work really hard to sort everything out on the trestle tables. Miss Stevenson was helping us. She'd got big pieces of card and marker pens so we could price everything, and she said it would be best to keep it simple and not to sell anything for more than five pounds, and some things at only one pound or fifty pence. "You don't want to be left with loads of stuff at the end, do you?" And she'd organized a float with plenty of change. Then gradually the clothes stopped arriving and, after a bit more sorting out, we were all ready for action, standing behind the tables like soldiers on guard.

But there wasn't any action and a little while later, Antonia looked at her watch. "It's past three o'clock and no one's here."

"They're probably giving us time to get organized," said Miss Stevenson. "Don't worry, they'll be here soon."

And she was right, because quite a few older Forest Ash girls trooped in shortly afterwards, and looked through all the clothes and things. One of them bought a bracelet for fifty pence, but the others didn't buy anything, which was disappointing. As they went out though, another handful of girls came in, and one of them spent ages deciding about a top. But in the end she didn't buy it, and I felt my disappointment starting to weigh me down again.

"Do you know where everyone is?" Miss Stevenson asked the girls who were just going out.

"Er, I think lots of people have gone to Jet's party," came the reply.

"Party?" said Bryony. "I thought that was yesterday."

"No, she decided to have it today in the end."

I looked at Bryony and saw fury in her eyes. She was obviously thinking what I was thinking – that Juliet had deliberately done this to spite me.

"Well, we don't all need to stay here with so few people around," said Miss Stevenson brightly. "Why don't we take turns to have breaks?"

So that's what happened. Antonia and Nicole took the first break, and while they were away hardly anyone came to the sale. Even Mrs. Pridham and Matron had gone off duty, so the place felt completely empty. It was Sasha and Izzy and Miss Stevenson herself who took the next break.

"I'll see if I can drum up a bit of custom. And perhaps the party will finish soon," she said, smiling encouragingly at Bryony and me as she left. And I had a sudden memory of another Sunday ages ago when I'd only been about seven and I'd stood at the front gate of our farmhouse with ten bunches of asparagus that I'd bundled up in rubber bands myself. I had a little table and a box for the money and I thought that ten cars would all come neatly along the road together, and see the scrawly *ASPARAGUS FOR SALE* sign that I'd written, and each stop to buy a bunch. But I'd stood there all afternoon, with my big brother coming to check on me every five minutes, and only a handful of cars even passed by, because we live on such a quiet road, and not one of them stopped. I remember that I didn't feel sad, just really confused, because I'd been so sure that what I'd imagined happening would actually happen.

Bryony and I were the last to take a break and the moment we were outside on our own I told her furiously that Jet made me sick. "I feel like going to Oakley and gatecrashing her party to tell her exactly what I think of her!"

Bryony put her arm round my shoulder for a moment and I felt her fingers gripping me tightly. "Poor Ems!" Then she let go and giggled. "You'd be like that nasty old fairy in the *Sleeping Beauty* story. You know – the one who goes stomping into the princess's christening party."

I imagined myself in a black cloak, swirling up to

Juliet. "I'd like to get that five-tiered cake of hers and crown her with it, you know!" I snapped.

Bryony creased up with laughter and could hardly walk because she found that so funny. But I was already striding off towards Oakley. I didn't really have any intention of going inside, because I knew *I'd* be the one to finish up looking a fool, not Juliet. But for some reason, I just wanted to see if there was any sign of the party. Knowing Jet, she'd probably invited the TV crew.

Once we got there, Bryony seemed uncomfortable. "Come on, Ems," she said. "We'd better be getting back, just in case..." She stopped talking and stared ahead of her towards the back door of Oakley. "Actually, isn't that Jet with a rubbish bag?"

I followed her gaze. Sure enough, Juliet was heading straight for the wheelie bins at the side of Oakley. Mel was following, also carrying a black bin liner.

"What do you think is in the bags?" I asked Bryony in a hiss, feeling a new layer of fury rising up inside me.

"Leftovers," Bryony replied. "The party must be over. Good. Maybe people will come to our sale now."

Then the next second, two more of Jet's friends came spilling out of the building, laughing and chatting, making their way across to the wheelie bins. One of them spotted us and must have said something to Jet, because the next minute she called out to us.

"Hey, you two! How did the clothes sale go? Did you make enough money for the 'worthy cause'?"

The sarcasm in her voice made the worst kind of prickles come out all over me and before I knew it, I'd marched right up to her.

"'Fraid you're a bit late for the party, Emily," she said mockingly.

I ignored that. "What's in the bag?"

She seemed to flinch for a second as though I'd hit her or something, but then she recovered instantly and I noticed her eyes turn nasty. "Well, let's take a look, shall we!" And with that she tipped the bin liner up so its contents spilled out all over the ground.

I looked with disgust at the mass of plastic beakers rolling and bobbing around, paper plates scattered amongst them.

"You weren't even going to bother recycling those, were you?" I said through clenched teeth. "You couldn't even be bothered to do that."

She laughed then, only it wasn't a proper laugh, more like a dry little snort. "Oh, just listen to her!

Doesn't she get on your nerves?" She turned to her friends and a few of them sniggered, but I didn't think they sounded very comfortable. "You're welcome to recycle the lot if you're so keen," Juliet went on, snatching the other bag off Mel and shaking it out dramatically. A mass of crumpled wrapping paper fell out amongst the cups and plates, before Juliet dropped the bin liners themselves and marched back inside. Her friends followed, but one or two of them looked back to where I was standing like a statue in the middle of the mess, and I noticed no one was laughing any more.

The moment the Oakley back door shut, I bent down and began stuffing the plates and wrapping paper into one bin liner, and the beakers into another, feeling my fingers getting sticky with dark chocolate icing and cake crumbs and pale globs of filling, and sweet fizzy drops of something that smelled of mint. It flashed through my mind that the paper plates might be okay to be torn up and used in the wormery, but then I remembered with a stab of sadness that of course we weren't *getting* a wormery any more.

"You ought to go back to Forest Ash," I said to Bryony when she tried to help me. "This won't take me a minute, honestly." I was determined not to appear anything except completely calm and matter-of-fact, just in case anyone was watching from a window, waiting to taunt me if I showed even a shred of self-pity.

"It's okay. I'll help you," Bryony said firmly.

But I wanted at least one of us to get back to the sale. "I'm fine, honestly. You go and explain to the others."

Bryony frowned, but I could tell she knew I wanted to be left alone. "Okay," she said, simply.

"I'll be there just as soon as I've done this."

So off she went and I carried on working, but it was taking me longer than I'd thought, because there was quite a bit of wind and the plastic cups kept rolling off. As I chased after one of them, I suddenly realized that someone had stopped it with their foot. I looked up to see one of the cameramen – the same one who I'd crashed into in the dining hall that time.

"Oh dear, had a bit of a spill?" he asked, sounding concerned. "Hang on a sec. Let me put this down and I'll give you a hand."

"It's all right, I've done most of it."

"Well, if you're sure."

I didn't say anything, and he kept filming.

"Someone had a party?"

"Uh-huh." I didn't feel like talking.

"Oh, right. And what are you doing with the rubbish?"

"Taking it to be recycled…" But then I realized I ought to clean all the globs of filling and icing off the plates first. "…When I've cleaned the plates."

I was stuffing the last few plates and cups into the bin liners when the man said, "So how come *you're* the only one doing the work?"

I shrugged and just said, "Dunno," but then I felt as though I was being a bit rude, so I tried to add a bit more, only it came out all stumbly and stupid. "I think it's…quite important…you know…to recycle stuff."

He didn't answer, but I noticed the camera never left me as I walked off with the bin liners banging against my legs. They weren't at all heavy, just awkward.

Five minutes later I walked into Forest Ash and got a shock, because the reception hall was teeming with people. Still lugging my bin liners, I wove a path through the middle of everyone and zoomed upstairs to the kitchen. I'd have to clean the plates up later. I just dumped the bags quickly, then went back down and along the corridor to the break-out room, where I found even more people. A quick glance at the tables told me that masses of stuff had been sold and all my friends were hard at work taking money and giving change.

"Wow! This is good!" I said, as I slotted in between Bryony and Sasha. "Where has everyone suddenly appeared from?"

Bryony grinned at me. "Jet's party, I guess!"

After that we stopped talking because there was too much work to do, and about twenty minutes later we'd sold everything except two tops and a bracelet, and although we hadn't counted the money, it looked like we'd made loads.

"Well done, girls!" said Miss Stevenson. "Mrs. Pridham will be proud of you."

I wasn't so sure that Mrs. Pridham would be proud of me personally, but at least she might be a little less cross with me now.

Chapter Ten

I'd decided to go and look for Stan at lunchtime on Monday, because of not being able to see him after school as I had to do detention. So the moment I finished my lunch I rushed straight over to the back of the kitchens, and as I drew near I heard the sound of an electric hedge-cutter, and felt so happy and relieved that he must be there, working in Ms. Carmichael's garden.

I hurried through the gate and across the old vegetable garden towards the gap in the hedge, but then I froze because the hedge-cutter had stopped and I could hear voices. It was impossible to tell what was being said, but one thing was for sure – the two people talking were Stan and Ms. Carmichael. I wasn't supposed to be round here any more now my gardening club had been taken away from me, and the last thing I wanted was to get into even more trouble. So I sneaked off, feeling more miserable than ever. What if Stan went to the garden to look ˙ for me after school and I wasn't there? He'd think I'd forgotten about him.

As fast as my legs would take me, I rushed off to find Bryony to ask her if she could go and explain to Stan after school about the stupid detention keeping me away, and find out if he'd be there the next day.

But Bryony was supposed to be going to another meeting about the Outward Bound course after classes and she'd forgotten to complete the form she had to fill in. She was planning to rush back to Forest Ash to get it, which would already be making her a bit late. She said she'd go as fast as she could, but she wasn't certain she'd have time to go to the garden. I could have asked one of the others, but they're not as brave and daring as Bryony and they might have felt as though they were trespassing after we'd been told that the gardening club was no more. I didn't want them to feel bad about saying no to me, so I just kept quiet and crossed my fingers like mad that Bryony might manage to fit it in after all.

It was so depressing going along to the library to do detention for Mrs. Egerton. I had to sit at the detention table, which was really embarrassing, because quite a few girls stared at me as if to say, *I wonder what she's done.* One of the Year Eleven students was supervising and Mrs. Egerton had given her the work that I was supposed to do, which was copying out all that I'd missed in the lesson plus three other paragraphs about democracy.

At first it was impossible to concentrate, because my mind kept on picturing Stan appearing from the gap in the hedge and looking round for me and not finding me there. It broke my heart that he might think I'd forgotten. I don't know how I managed to copy out any of the stupid history – I just felt useless and utterly helpless.

Every so often the Year Eleven girl came over to my table to check that I was doing what I was supposed to be doing, and once or twice her friends came in and they had a quick chat in whispers. Maybe they were just trying to make it less boring for her. I had to admit it seemed rather unfair that a student had to stay behind to supervise my detention – almost as bad as doing the detention yourself.

But then someone else came to talk to her, and this time I could tell it wasn't just a friend. A girl was giving her a message that was something to do with me, because they both looked in my direction, and I got a bad feeling about the grave expressions they were wearing.

The girl supervising came over and bobbed down beside me. "You've got to go and see Ms. Carmichael."

I gulped.

"Just give me your work. It doesn't matter that it's not finished. I'll explain to Mrs. Egerton."

I stood up on shaky legs and felt the colour draining from my face.

"Do you know where to go?" she asked.

I shook my head.

"You go to the main building and knock on the door marked *School Office*. Ms. Carmichael's private secretary will show you from there."

As I walked out of the library and along the corridor to go outside, I felt sick. Ms. Carmichael must have somehow seen me in the garden at lunchtime through the hedge. What if she expelled me? What would Mum and Dad say? If only, if only, if only I could rewind the whole week and start all over again.

My footsteps in the hall of the main building

sounded so loud and so did my knock on the door of the office.

"I've come to see Ms. Carmichael," I said in a thin wobbly voice when someone opened the door.

"Ah, yes. Follow me, please." She wasn't smiling. "Are you the girl Ms. Carmichael's expecting?"

"Yes," I managed to croak.

"So you are...?"

"Emily Dowd."

We went down a corridor I'd never been down before and she tapped lightly on a door which said *Ms. Carmichael, Headmistress*. Then she leaned her head against the door as though she had to strain to hear the reply.

"Right, in you go," she said a moment later. Then she pushed open the door and said, "Emily Dowd to see you, Ms. Carmichael."

"Come in please, Emily."

I don't know how my shaky legs managed to follow that simple instruction and I kept my eyes on Ms. Carmichael's face right up until she told me to sit down at the other side of her table. I was searching for clues about just how cross she was, but I couldn't tell at all.

"Now, Emily..." She paused and I felt my heart turn over, because it was as though she couldn't

141

think what on earth to say to someone who'd done as many bad things as I had. "Miss Gerard came to see me today. I understand you approached her about the school changing its catering policy?"

Her eyes were like magnets. I tried to look away but I couldn't, so I nodded dumbly and felt my cheeks draining of colour as I prayed that she'd get straight to the telling-off, so then I could find out if I'd been expelled or not.

"And Miss Gerard told you that the school had no plans for such a change?"

She was getting nearer. In fact I could even hear the next words coming: *And yet you still went ahead and made gardening an excuse for missing lessons...*

I didn't even nod this time, just waited for the worst.

"Well, I've seen what you've done in the old kitchen garden..."

I swallowed. "Sorry."

"...And I must say I'm quite impressed. It was Stan who first told me about your interest in the garden, and as Miss Gerard and the governors and I had been only recently in discussion about what to do with the land, it seemed like quite a coincidence that one of the students was showing such an interest."

Ms. Carmichael was talking away and I felt numb. I didn't get what she was saying. Why hadn't she got round to the part where I got expelled?

"I've been keeping an eye on the footage from the production company's filming, and that prompted me to talk to Mrs. Pridham..."

Did she mean the filming of me gardening?

"I know you've been in trouble recently, Emily, but Mrs. Pridham is convinced that it's all because you're so passionate about gardening and wanting to help the environment. Would that be a fair comment?"

I couldn't take everything in. I didn't know what to say. My mind was spinning.

Would it be a fair comment? What had Mrs. Pridham said? That I'm *passionate about gardening and wanting to help the environment*. Somehow I managed to latch on to that bit and hold it in my mind. Yes, yes I *was* passionate. Still I didn't trust myself to speak though, so I just nodded.

"Don't look so worried, Emily. I'm not a monster." She broke into a smile. "Just try and tell me what you think. Miss Gerard said you were very sure of yourself. She was really bowled over by the way you expressed your feelings, but you caught her at a time when she was very busy with other things.

Miss Gerard is a very thorough person, however, and later that day she went back over what you'd said, in her mind, and really saw the potential in it. She told me she truly thinks that with a strong committee of students and teachers dedicated to the cause, we can change things around and go back to buying in much less fresh produce and growing much more of it ourselves."

I was totally amazed. I couldn't believe my ears. But I had to be quite sure...

"So you're...not exactly...telling me off?" I managed to stutter.

She laughed then. "I'm not telling you off at all, Emily. I'm just checking that you still feel as strongly as you did when you spoke to Miss Gerard..."

It was as though someone had taken a gag off my mouth and I could breathe and I could speak and I was free. "I'll never ever change how I feel, Ms. Carmichael," I said in a voice that sounded suddenly a bit too loud for the room. "All I care about is nature and the cycle of the seasons and the earth and the way we live. The secret is keeping in tune with nature."

Ms. Carmichael nodded and blinked several times. It reminded me of how I'd done exactly the same thing after I'd seen Mrs. Pridham, only that was because I'd been trying to stop more tears from spilling out.

"Yes...yes, that's right," she said quietly. "Now, I've spoken to Tony and also to Stan, and the good news is that Stan is happy to head up the gardening team and to be in charge of the project. I know from what I've seen that you're a hard worker, Emily, and hopefully you'll get lots of help if you restart your gardening club..." She paused and did a few more blinks, then her voice turned brisker. "But of course we've got the holidays to consider, not to mention lessons, so it'll be ideal to have Stan overseeing the plot."

I felt like giving Ms. Carmichael a big hug, because the words she'd just said were the best words I thought I'd ever, ever heard. But for some unknown reason, even though I was so happy, I actually found myself crying, and then Ms. Carmichael came round to me and patted my shoulder.

"I hope these are tears of happiness?" she said.

And I couldn't even speak for crying but I managed to nod, and she went back round to her own side of the table and spoke into her phone to ask her secretary for two cups of tea. I felt my brain split into three parts then. One part wanted to drink the tea and talk some more about the wonderful new project that was going to happen, one part wanted to run all the way back to Forest Ash and tell Bryony and the others what had happened, and the last part wanted to dance on Ms. Carmichael's table and to scream out, "I did it!"

A few days later it was announced that the production company were going to film one final special assembly before they left. I couldn't help feeling a bit sad. It was just the thought that it was the end of their time with us, and I don't like endings. I prefer things to keep turning round and round in cycles.

As we all filed into the hall, the first thing we noticed was that it looked extra bright with the lights that the film crew had erected. Apart from that, nothing seemed different, because we were so used to seeing cameras around now that we didn't really take much notice of them.

I thought about what a lot had happened since that other special assembly when Ms. Carmichael had made her announcement about the film crew coming to Silver Spires. It seemed such a long time ago. My friends all said it was amazing that I'd been through so much in such a short time. And I was still in shock about the way everything had turned out.

After my meeting with Ms. Carmichael, I'd called a truth talk in the dorm and we'd all piled onto my bed, where I'd told the whole story of my happy ending in big detail. I love thinking back to how my friends had kept gasping, then breaking into cheers and bursting into applause, and Bryony had seemed like the proudest of them all. I'd been really touched, because it turned out she'd even made herself late for her meeting by going to see Stan after all, and giving him my message.

Then the next day I'd raced over to the garden and found him waiting for me, wearing the biggest grin ever. He'd said straight away how pleased he was that he'd got a proper project to get his teeth into, especially as now he didn't have to leave Silver Spires after all, which he'd been dreading after such a long time working here. We'd sat down on the little wall just inside the hedge and talked and talked about all the things we planned on growing in the garden and how we were going to try getting lots of other girls interested in the club.

And thinking about that now, coming into the hall, made tears prick the backs of my eyes again. But then I got a shock, because sitting next to Miss Gerard, in a suit and tie and shiny shoes, was Stan himself. He must have been looking out for me, because our eyes met and he gave me a massive smile. And straight after that I got another shock, because right beside him was Emily Peters. She actually stood up and gave me a little wave when she saw me, which made me feel so happy.

When everyone was seated, Ms. Carmichael began to talk. "It hardly seems a minute since we were all gathered in here for me to tell you the important news about the film crew, and now they're about to leave us. But before they go we're in for a treat, because we're actually going to see an extract or two from the footage right now!"

There was a big wave of gasps and a few "Oh no"s spoken in cringing voices, and one big "Yes!"

That was Juliet, and because her voice had stood out, quite a few people turned to look at her, including me, and I noticed she went a bit red. Personally, I was thinking it might be quite interesting to see some bits of film, as long as there wasn't any of me, which there wouldn't be, as I'd hardly been filmed at all.

"So now I'm going to hand over to Mark from the crew," went on Ms. Carmichael. She started off the clapping as the man called Mark went up to the platform at the front, and I saw that he was the same cameraman who'd been there that awful time when I'd been scooping up the cups and plates from Juliet's party.

"Thank you, everyone," Mark began. "It should be me clapping you lot, because you've done well to put up with cameras popping up all over the place for the last couple of weeks. As you know, we're doing a programme about your school – its past, its present and its future – and we've certainly found it tremendously interesting here at Silver Spires. As soon as we know the date that the programme will be aired I'll let Ms. Carmichael know, but it won't be in the next couple of months." A big groan of disappointment went round the hall when he said that and then we all laughed at ourselves, which made Mark laugh too.

"We don't normally give anyone sneak previews of what we've filmed, but the reason we're making an exception today is because Ms. Carmichael specially requested it, so I'm handing back to you, Ms. Carmichael."

Mark left the platform and Ms. Carmichael went back to the centre. "I wanted to show you, girls," she began in a serious voice, "how if you really believe in something from the bottom of your heart and you feel strongly enough about it to want to do something, you *can* make a difference. Each and every one of you can. And we have someone here at Silver Spires who has done just that. One of our youngest students has helped convince the staff and myself that it's time we went back to a greener way of life." My heart lurched and I found myself blushing and wishing Ms. Carmichael would stop now. But she was carrying on and it was only bearable because Bryony had reached for my hand and was holding it tight. "Now you might think there's a lot of loose talk about being green. And so there is, which is why Miss Gerard, our domestic bursar, didn't pay much attention to this student at first. But actually putting that talk into action is a different matter. Now at this point, I'd like to introduce Emily Peters, who came to Silver Spires fifty years ago as a student."

Everyone clapped politely as Emily walked briskly onto the stage.

"I'm not going to say very much at all, girls, because I know you want to get on with watching the film extracts. But let me tell you this. The girl on the film has impressed me more than any other girl I know, past or present. And it makes my heart sing to think that this school might once again return to its old values."

Emily nodded firmly and Stan began a new wave of clapping as she went back to her seat beside him.

Ms. Carmichael stood up again. "You've all heard the saying 'actions speak louder than words'. Well, now we're going to see an example of that." Then she nodded at Mark and moved to one side as an enlargement of Stan's old photo of his tall green garden was projected onto the wall at the front. After a few seconds it was gone, and in its place was the garden as it looks now.

I heard a few gasps and then there was silence and the camera angle slowly moved, and the next gasp came out of my mouth, because there was me, digging the soil. I thought I'd be embarrassed to see myself, and I don't know whether it was because of the stillness in the hall, but it seemed as though everyone was taking it seriously, which was a big relief. I felt Bryony's fingers squeezing my own tight as I watched myself working away.

Suddenly the shot changed to one of me bending down and scooping up those paper plates and plastic cups. Then we heard Mark's voice on the film.

"Someone had a party?"

"Uh-huh."

"Oh, right. And what are you doing with the rubbish?"

"*Taking it to be recycled... When I've cleaned the plates.*"

"*So how come* you're *the only one doing the work?*"

"*Dunno... I think it's...quite important...you know... to recycle stuff.*"

I glanced sideways and noticed Juliet's embarrassed eyes, then looked back at the film. The next thing we saw was me walking right into the distance with the bin liners, on and on and on, with not a sound. And there wasn't a sound in the hall either, but Bryony was still squeezing my hand tight, thank goodness. And then the film suddenly stopped and Ms. Carmichael was back in the middle of the platform again.

"Emily, would you like to come up, please?" she said quietly.

And my heart banged against my ribs as I slowly got up. Then, as I began to walk to the front, the whole hall burst into applause, which made the hairs on my arms stand on end.

"I won't ask you to make a speech or anything," said Ms. Carmichael, which was a big relief, because there was no way I'd be able to speak to the whole school. I was far too nervous. "But Mrs. Pridham has something to say, I think."

And then Mrs. Pridham came out to the front

and stood beside me. "I've actually got something to show you. You have Miss Gerard to thank for this. After I mentioned your original plan for the money raised at your clothes sale, she persuaded me that this was just what the school needs." Mrs. Pridham gave a little chuckle as she lifted pieces of cardboard off some sort of box that had been on the platform all the time, but which I hadn't really paid any attention to. And there, right before my eyes, was a huge wormery.

"Oh, thank you! It's amazing, Mrs. Pridham! I can't believe it!"

Mrs. Pridham looked as happy as I felt, but lots of people were calling out to ask what it was.

"You explain, Emily," whispered Mrs. Pridham.

So I did.

"Thank you, everyone, for coming to our clothes sale," I began. "With the money that we raised we've bought this wormery. There are about five hundred composting worms in here…" One or two people made disgusted noises, but I just ignored them and carried on. "The way it works is that you throw in apple cores or banana peel, and even things like the hair from your hairbrushes, and newspaper and stuff, and the worms will make the best ever compost, which will help the new vegetables to grow in the garden, and the peelings will be recycled into compost too, and so it will go…on and on. Everything in nature works in cycles like this and the secret is to keep in tune with nature's plan. And Silver Spires will be helping that cycle. It will be truly… recycling."

I stopped and looked at Mrs. Pridham to see if that was all right and she broke into a big beaming smile, and then someone was clapping, and I looked across to see Stan standing up and clapping his hands right out in front of him, as though he was trying to reach all the way to me. The next minute, everyone was joining in. I tried to find Bryony's face in the sea of faces in front of me, but all I could see was Juliet. I noticed her cheeks were very red as her eyes met mine.

"Can I go?" I asked Mrs. Pridham, which made her laugh for some reason.

Ms. Carmichael then raised her hand for silence and asked for a show of hands, so she could get a rough idea of how many people would be interested in joining me in my gardening club. "There will be a sheet on the noticeboard in the main reception hall for everyone who is interested to sign their name."

Immediately, it seemed like at least half the school raised their hands, even the teachers. And that was when I saw that one of the other cameramen was filming away, and I realized that he had been recording all through the whole assembly.

As I made my way back to my friends, loads of people kept patting me on the back and congratulating me as I passed.

"This is mad! I feel like a film star or something," I whispered to Bryony when I was finally back beside her and everyone had sat down again.

"You *are*," was all she said. My best friend never says loads of words when two will do.

This time I squeezed *her* hand. And inside my shaky self, my heart squeezed with happiness as I thought about Mum and Dad watching the film.

From little seeds grow big results.

Yes! I'd actually made it happen.

Emily's Top Ten Eco Tips

Growing your own veg is just one way of helping to
protect our fab planet. Here are my top ten tips for
being a gorgeously green girl!

★ Invest in a cool canvas shopping bag and
say goodbye to nasty non-biodegradable plastic.

★ Don't throw your old clothes out to rot
in landfill sites. Donate them to charity
shops, or swap them with your friends
for a fun – and free – new look!

★ Always recycle paper, glass and cans and check
for the recycling symbol on your plastic. Try to buy
products made using recycled materials too.

★ Get on your bike! It's greener and cheaper
than getting lifts in cars or catching the bus all the
time, plus you'll get fit too!

★ Save water by turning the tap off in between
gulps when you're brushing your teeth.

★ If you get a new mobile phone, remember to recycle your old one – many charity shops will take them, and it stops chemicals from the phone ending up in the earth.

★ If you're not using your TV or computer, turn it off – a computer monitor left on overnight wastes enough energy to microwave six dinners!

★ Think twice before asking your parents to turn the heating up. Try sticking on an extra-cosy jumper and some snuggly socks instead.

★ Why not adopt or sponsor an endangered animal for yourself, or as a present for your friends? You'll often get cute pics, and a certificate too.

★ Never, *ever* litter. It can harm animals, damages the environment and it looks...well, rubbish.

If everyone does their little bit to look after our amazing planet, we can really make a difference. Good luck, green girls!

Emily

Complete your
School Friends
collection!

First Term at Silver Spires   ISBN 9780746072240
Katy's nervous about going to boarding school for the first time – especially with the big secret she has to hide.

Drama at Silver Spires   ISBN 9780746072257
Georgie's desperate to get her favourite part in the school play, but she's up against some stiff competition.

Rivalry at Silver Spires   ISBN 9780746072264
Grace is eager to win in the swimming gala for Hazeldean – until someone starts sending mean messages about her.

Princess at Silver Spires   ISBN 9780746089576
Naomi hates being the centre of attention, but when she's asked to model for a charity fashion show, she can't say no.

Secrets at Silver Spires   ISBN 9780746089583
Jess is struggling with her schoolwork and has to have special classes, but she can't bear to tell her friends the truth.

Star of Silver Spires   ISBN 9780746089590
Mia longs to enter a song she's written in the Silver Spires Star contest, but she's far too scared to perform onstage.

Party at Silver Spires   ISBN 9780746098646
Nicole's determined to keep her scholarship a secret, in case it stops her from making friends with her dorm.

Dancer at Silver Spires   ISBN 9780746098653
Izzy's trying to put her hopes of becoming a ballerina behind her – until the school puts on a dance show.

Dreams at Silver Spires   ISBN 9780746098660
Emily dreams of starting a cool club at school...but first she must persuade the teachers she's got what it takes.

Magic at Silver Spires   ISBN 9780746098677
Antonia and her friends must prove to her parents that she belongs at Silver Spires...before they take her back to Italy!

Success at Silver Spires   ISBN 9780746098684
Sasha is delighted when she discovers her natural talent for sports, but she faces tough competition from a rival.

Mystery at Silver Spires   ISBN 9780746098691
Bryony keeps hearing spooky noises in the night. Is the school haunted, or has the dorm got an unexpected guest?

Want to know more about the
Silver Spires girls?

Or try a quiz to discover which
School Friend you're most like?

You can even send Silver Spires e-cards
to your best friends and post your own
book reviews online!

It's all at

www.silverspiresschool.co.uk

Check it out now!

For more fun and friendship-packed reads
go to **www.fiction.usborne.com**